Holly's gaze met his, and for a moment she thought he was going to lean over and kiss her.

If he did, there was no way she could stop herself from kissing him back, baby or no baby. She wanted him. Really, really wanted him.

She felt her mouth parting, and her skin tingled all over with anticipation. Her lower lip felt super-sensitive.

He reached out and rubbed the pad of his thumb against her lower lip, and excitement coiled deep in her belly. Everything was forgotten except this moment, this feeling, this connection. She was dimly aware of Harry propping the cello against the piano, and then somehow he was sitting next to her on the piano stool, his arms were wrapped around her waist, her fingers were tangled in his hair and her wrists resting against the nape of his neck, and he was kissing her—*really* kissing her.

And it felt like fireworks going off overhead. Sparkles of silver and pink and gold.

When he broke the kiss, she was shaking. It felt really familiar—but how could it?

Dear Reader,

I've never written an "amnesia" book before, so I set myself a challenge to write one I could believe. What happens if you have a wild fling with someone, something happens to make you lose all your memories of even meeting them and then you meet them again?

When cellist Harry meets archaeologist Holly (you have no idea how hard it was to stop myself from calling her Sally), they have the fun of falling in love all over again a second time—with some added complications.

The book is set partly in Bath, a place I hugely enjoyed visiting with my daughter (especially the Roman baths and the Herschel museum), partly in Cambridge and partly in London. If you like Regency, roses, Romans and ruins, you'll enjoy this. Oh, and lakes and swans. (Put those last two together—yup, some of the soundtrack is from my Friday ballet class!)

I loved writing this book, and I hope you enjoy Holly and Harry's story. I also hope you'll enjoy the music, especially the nod to one of my all-time favorite films. Though hopefully this book will make you smile rather than sob buckets, as said film does to me!

With love,

Kate Hardy

One Night to Remember

Kate Hardy

H⊛ **HARLEQUIN**®

Romance™

Recycling programs
for this product may
not exist in your area.

ISBN-13: 978-1-335-55619-6

One Night to Remember

Copyright © 2020 by Pamela Brooks

All rights reserved. No part of this book may be used or reproduced in
any manner whatsoever without written permission except in the case of
brief quotations embodied in critical articles and reviews.

This is a work of fiction. Names, characters, places and incidents
are either the product of the author's imagination or are used fictitiously.
Any resemblance to actual persons, living or dead, businesses,
companies, events or locales is entirely coincidental.

This edition published by arrangement with Harlequin Books S.A.

For questions and comments about the quality of this book,
please contact us at CustomerService@Harlequin.com.

Harlequin Enterprises ULC
22 Adelaide St. West, 40th Floor
Toronto, Ontario M5H 4E3, Canada
www.Harlequin.com

Printed in U.S.A.

Kate Hardy has always loved books and could read before she went to school. She discovered Harlequin books when she was twelve and decided this was what she wanted to do. When she isn't writing, Kate enjoys reading, cinema, ballroom dancing and the gym. You can contact her via her website, katehardy.com.

Books by Kate Hardy

Harlequin Romance

A Crown by Christmas

Soldier Prince's Secret Baby Gift

Summer at Villa Rosa

The Runaway Bride and the Billionaire

His Shy Cinderella
Christmas Bride for the Boss
Reunited at the Altar
A Diamond in the Snow
Finding Mr. Right in Florence

Harlequin Medical Romance

Miracles at Muswell Hill Hospital

Christmas with Her Daredevil Doc
Their Pregnancy Gift

Unlocking the Italian Doc's Heart
Carrying the Single Dad's Baby
Heart Surgeon, Prince...Husband!
A Nurse and a Pup to Heal Him
Mistletoe Proposal on the Children's Ward

Visit the Author Profile page
at Harlequin.com for more titles.

For Julia, my editor—who is simply a joy to
work with—with love

Praise for
Kate Hardy

"Ms. Hardy has written a very sweet novel about
forgiveness and breaking the molds we place
ourselves in...a good heartstring novel that will
have you embracing happiness in your heart."

—*Harlequin Junkie* on *Christmas Bride for the Boss*

CHAPTER ONE

'THE BEST WAY to get over someone is to have a mad fling,' Natalie said.

'I don't need a fling,' Holly protested.

And it still felt too soon after Simon. Besides, how could a one-night stand take the place of eight years of being with someone? She'd thought their relationship was strong enough to cope with him being on secondment in New York for six months. Holly usually spent most of the summer away somewhere on a dig, coming home for weekends, and that had always been fine. She and Simon had rubbed along without any problems. They'd been happy.

Or so she'd believed. The more she thought about it, the more she realised how wrong she'd been.

Simon had met Fenella in New York, fallen hopelessly in love with her, and called off his wedding to Holly at the end of his secondment—only a month before they had been due to walk down the aisle together. He'd left it to Holly to cancel all the wedding preparations and send back the wedding gifts with an apologetic note, on the grounds that she was better at that sort of thing than he was; she'd gritted her teeth and done it simply so she knew everything had been sorted out rather than Simon dragging his feet and leaving something undone.

And, although his offer to buy out Holly's share of their house meant that she didn't have all the hassle of trying to sell the house, it hurt that he wanted to share *their* house with someone else. Plus she had had to find somewhere else to live, though Natalie had stepped in immediately with an offer of her spare room until Holly could find somewhere suitable.

The last fortnight had been particularly hideous. Holly had seemed to spend the whole time alternately apologising and squirming, knowing that everyone was gossiping about the situation behind her back. Some people were kind, though she'd hated being pigeon-holed as the dumped fiancée. The pitying looks were hard to take. Thankfully the veneer of politeness stopped people actually asking what was wrong with her and why

Simon had been so quick to fall for someone else, but she knew they were thinking it.

And she'd had to go through all their things and divvy them up; though, once she'd started, she'd realised how few of their joint belongings had been chosen by her, or even together. How had she let herself be such a doormat? Why hadn't she said no to Simon more often, or insisted on having more of *her* choices? What a fool she'd been.

Holly had honestly believed that Simon had loved her. She'd loved him, too. OK, so it hadn't been the big grand passion she'd read about in novels or seen at the movies, with rainbows and starbursts and fanfares every time he'd kissed her, but she knew she was plain and ordinary, so she'd never really expected to have that sort of relationship. She and Simon had liked each other at their first meeting and they'd got on well together. They'd dated, moved in together, bought a house. They'd been *happy*.

But not quite happy enough, it seemed.

Because in New York Simon had met the woman who really was his big grand passion, the one who made fireworks go off in his head when he kissed her—something that Holly had clearly never managed to do—and everything had fallen apart.

Maybe if Holly had been the real love of his life, they would've got married years ago, and they wouldn't have kept finding excuses to wait a bit longer before the wedding. Buying a house together rather than spending all that money on a party had seemed the sensible thing to do, given that house prices were going up so quickly. And then they'd both been busy with their careers. It was really only last year, when Simon's mum had asked some very pointed questions about just when her son was planning to settle down properly and produce some grandchildren, that Simon and Holly had set the date for their wedding. Even then, they'd set it for a year in the future rather than rushing into it.

As Fenella was apparently too green with morning sickness right now to get on a plane, Simon's mum was going to get her much-wanted grandchildren very soon, whereas Holly's mum would just have to make do with the grandchildren she had. And Holly wasn't going to let herself think about the children she and Simon might have had. The child she'd secretly started to want six months ago, when Simon had first gone to America. *The child Simon had made without her.*

'You need a holiday,' Natalie said.

'I'm fine.' Holly had cancelled her leave,

not wanting to take the week's holiday that should've been her honeymoon. A honeymoon for one surely had to be the most unappealing thing ever. Or maybe it was better than going on honeymoon with someone who didn't really love you. Wasn't it better to be alone than to be with someone who didn't want you or value you?

And why hadn't she realised sooner that Simon had fallen out of love with her and that being together had become a habit instead of what they'd both really wanted?

'Anyway, it gives me time to concentrate on my career,' she said, trying to find a positive and damp down her feelings of misery and loneliness.

'Dry bones.' Natalie rolled her eyes.

'Sometimes they're wet,' Holly pointed out, 'if they're at the bottom of a rain-filled trench.'

Natalie shuddered. 'Cold, wet and muddy. Give me my nice warm kitchen at the magazine any day. Even if I do have an over-fussy art director wanting me to make a little tweak here and there that actually means making the whole dish all over again for the photographer.' She looked at Holly. 'Holls, if you're spending all your time with the bones of people who died centuries ago, you're never going to meet anyone else. Archaeologists aren't sexy.'

Holly laughed. 'Of course they are. What about Indiana Jones?'

'He's a fantasy.'

'All right, then. Brendan Fraser in *The Mummy*. You have to admit he's utterly gorgeous.'

'Fantasy again,' Natalie said. 'In real life, your male colleagues are either like Gandalf, muttering into their very grey, very straggly beards, or they're total nerds who are terrified at the thought of talking to a real live woman.'

'Apart from the fact that's a horrible sweeping generalisation, it's also not true. My male colleagues all talk to me,' Holly said.

'They work with you, so they see you as safe, not as a woman,' Natalie pointed out.

Which Holly knew was true. And she tried not to mind or let it make her feel even more inadequate than Simon had already made her feel. Why wasn't she the sort of woman that a man fell hopelessly in love with?

'You do need a break, though. I know you're not busy this weekend—' because it would've been her hen weekend, which Holly had also cancelled—'so let's go to Bath. It's the next best thing to Rome. You can drool over the curse tablets at the Roman Baths, and I can drag you off for afternoon tea in the Pump Room. And in between we can go and sigh over the lovely Georgian houses in the Circus.'

'And you can see how many Mr Darcy-alikes you can spot?' Holly teased, knowing her best friend well. Natalie was a complete Austen addict.

'Something like that,' Natalie said with a smile.

'All right. Actually, it'll be nice to go away with you,' Holly admitted. She hadn't been looking forward to moping at home this weekend. The last weekend in the house she'd shared with Simon, because next week she was moving her few possessions into a rented flat in Camden and he was moving back from his mother's to their house.

'Good, because I've already booked the hotel.'

Holly winced. 'That's a risky strategy, Nat. What if I'd said no?'

'Then I would've guilt-tripped you into coming with me,' Natalie said with a grin. 'Life's too short not to take the odd risk. We're staying in the middle of Bath, and according to all the review sites our hotel does the best breakfast ever. And this one is on me,' she added, 'because I know how much you were looking forward to Rome. It was the nearest thing I could think of, because I was guessing that Rome itself might have been too much to bear, even if I'd booked a different hotel.'

Holly hugged her. 'Thank you. That's really kind of you.'

'It's exactly what you would've done for me, if I'd been in your shoes,' Natalie reminded her. 'I still think Simon's the biggest idiot ever. The way he treated you—you deserved a lot better than that.'

Yeah. It would've been nice if he'd broken up with her *before* making Fenella pregnant. That was the bit that really hurt. Why had he kept stringing her along when he clearly didn't love her any more? Why had he let her believe that everything was just fine? Though it wasn't all him: why hadn't she seen the problems for herself?

And she hated the way people treated her as The Woman Who'd Been Cheated On. The whispered conversations that stopped when she walked into a room. The judgements. The friends taking sides. People they'd both known since university, who'd been her friends before she'd met Simon, had thrown in their lot with him; it had made her feel even more worthless, despite the fact she knew she was better off without them. She hadn't been enough as a partner, and she hadn't been enough as a friend.

How could she not have noticed their relationship unravelling? The signs must've been there before he'd gone to New York. She'd managed to snatch just one weekend with Simon during his secondment, quite early on, and he'd been distracted throughout it. He'd said it was work when she asked him; but now she knew it had been Fenella distracting him.

'At least he didn't dump me at the altar,' Holly said, keeping her tone light. 'It could've been a lot worse.'

'It could've been a lot *better.*' Natalie rolled her eyes. 'You're too nice for your own good.'

'Believe you me, I'm not being nice. I'm hurt and I'm angry, and bits of me want to punch him and yell and scream. But having a tantrum isn't going to change things,' Holly said. 'Simon doesn't love me any more, and having a hissy fit isn't going to make him decide he does love me after all. I don't want to be in a relationship where I'm the one who loves the other the most. I hate feeling so pathetic.'

'But you still love him.'

Bits of her did, and bits of her didn't. 'Eight

years is a long time to be with someone,' Holly said. 'And most of them were good years.' But the other thing that nagged at her was how much of it had been her fault. If she'd made Simon feel loved and appreciated enough, instead of taking him for granted, maybe he would've acknowledged that he fancied Fenella but he wouldn't actually have done anything about it. Those six months of physical distance had turned all too quickly into emotional distance. 'I guess somewhere along the way we started drifting apart, and I should've been paying more attention to him.' It was the first time she'd acknowledged it to someone else, though the thoughts had kept her awake at night.

'He should've been paying just as much attention to *you*,' Natalie countered.

Maybe—but he hadn't. Holly shrugged. 'It feels pretty crap right now, but I'll live. Don't worry, I'm not going to turn into Miss Havisham or anything like that.'

'Good, because Simon isn't worth it.' Natalie squeezed her hand. 'OK. We'll get the train on Friday after work, do the Roman Baths first thing on Saturday morning, go for a walk to look at all the gorgeous houses, have afternoon tea at the Pump Room—and then, dear Cinders, you shall go to the ball.'

'Ball? What ball?' Holly asked.

'I got us tickets for a ball on Saturday night. It's just outside Bath—in an Elizabethan manor house, which you'll love. And it's Regency dress.'

'Regency dress?' Holly groaned. 'So this *is* all about your Darcy obsession.'

Natalie gave her an unrepentant grin. 'Asking you wouldn't have worked, so I'm dragging you out to have some fun.'

Holly grimaced. 'I love you, Nat, and I do appreciate what you've done for me, but a ball isn't really my idea of fun. I've got two left feet. And as for dressing up, the cost—'

'Problem solved, before you say you don't have a dress. I've already hired one for you,' Natalie informed her.

'What? How? It might not fit.'

Natalie coughed. 'If it fits me, it fits you. Someone on the magazine knows a really good hire place, and I went to see them yesterday. I tried on a few dresses and the ones I got for us are fabulous.'

'Uh-huh.'

'Holls, if nothing else, you'll enjoy the music. Apparently there's a brilliant string quartet who are going to play on a floating bandstand in the middle of the lake. So if you just want to sit and listen to them and sip

Pimm's and watch the sunset and not even put a single foot into the ballroom, that's fine by me.'

Holly knew her best friend was trying to distract her from the train wreck of her personal life, coming up with ideas to keep her busy. And she appreciated it, because otherwise she rather thought she'd start to get really insecure and ask just what was so wrong with her that Simon hadn't wanted her any more. She'd always known she'd been punching well above her weight—Simon looked more like a film star than an accountant—and when Holly had stalked Fenella on social media she'd discovered that the other woman was super-glamorous.

Fenella was everything Holly herself wasn't. No wonder Simon had fallen head over heels with her. If you put a scruffy archaeologist who wore ancient jeans and T-shirts and usually had a smear of mud on her face from the trench she was working in next to someone with perfect hair and make-up and a designer suit, it was obvious who'd win in the gorgeousness stakes. Who'd be *enough*.

'I'll set foot in the ballroom,' Holly promised, 'so you get a chance to do some dancing. And I appreciate you having my back.'

'Always,' Natalie said fiercely. 'You've

been my best friend since we were eleven. That's not going to change. I'm quite prepared to fly over to New York and beat Simon over the head with an umbrella—and threaten to baste Fenella in the stickiest marinade and barbecue her.'

Holly couldn't help smiling. 'Thank you, but there are better things to do in New York.'

Natalie gave her an 'are you insane?' stare. 'Can I at least make a mini-Simon out of modelling clay and stick pins into him?'

'That's money,' Holly said, 'you could spend more satisfyingly on posh gin.'

'Oh, the modelling clay and pins would be satisfying enough,' Natalie said. 'But you're right. Posh gin's a good idea. And we are *so* having posh gin at the ball. So I'll meet you at Paddington Station at four o'clock on Friday—next to the Paddington Bear bench—and we'll get the next train to Bath.' She smiled. 'I've got our tickets. I'll send you the email so you've got the PDF of our tickets, too, just in case something goes wrong with my phone.'

'It's more likely to be me forgetting to charge my phone. You know how hopeless I am,' Holly said wryly. 'You're the best friend ever. Thanks, Nat.'

'Roman archaeology, afternoon tea and a

Regency ball. That's all our favourite things covered,' Natalie said with a smile.

'And no matchmaking,' Holly said, mindful of her best friend's views about how to get over a broken relationship. 'Just a nice girly weekend. You and me.'

'A nice girly weekend. You and me,' Natalie echoed.

Wine plus his parents really wasn't a good combination, Harry thought. He was really glad that that his brother Dominic, his sister Ellen and their partners were here, too. It was the only thing that made a visit to Beauchamp Abbey bearable. He wished the meal had been Sunday lunch rather than Saturday dinner, because having small children around might have dampened the sniping a bit.

Then again, the sniping had been there when he'd been a small child, too. It had grown worse over the years, and it had been truly unbearable when Dom and Nell had both been at university. Harry hadn't been able to keep the peace between his parents and he'd hated all the conflict, so he'd escaped to his grandmother's as much as possible. His parents' behaviour had gone a long way to putting him off the idea of ever getting married.

At least Ellen had asked him to stay with her, so he didn't have to put up with a whole weekend of their parents. Now, with the cheese course over, his father was making inroads into the brandy and getting really snippy. 'You're thirty now, Harry. Isn't it about time you got married again and settled down properly?' George asked.

Trust his father not to pull his punches. And considering that Viscount Moran had made it very clear that Harry's ex-wife was much too lower class for his son... Harry damped down the anger. Having difficult in-laws wasn't the only reason, or even one of the main reasons, why he and Rochelle had broken up. But it hadn't helped.

'I'm a bit busy with my career, Pa,' he said as blandly as he could. 'It's not fair to ask someone to wait about for me when I'm touring so much.' And if marriage hadn't worked with someone who was in the same business and understood that you had to travel a lot to make a living out of music, it definitely wasn't going to work with someone who'd be left at home all the time.

'I think we've given you your head for quite long enough, letting you mess around with your cello for all these years,' George said. 'It's way past time you came back here, settled down and pulled your weight in the family business.'

'Messing around' wasn't quite how Harry would describe graduating from the Royal Academy of Music with first-class honours, or working with a renowned string quartet for the last six years. Not to mention the fact that he'd paid for the repairs of the conservatory roof at the abbey last year. He did his share of supporting the family estate, except he did it from as much distance as he thought he could get away with.

And it was getting harder and harder to bite his tongue. He knew his father resented the fact that Harry had gone his own way, but did George always have to bring it up and try to make his youngest son feel as if his career was worthless and he was a useless son? But, much as he wanted to stand up to his father's bullying and tell him where to get off, Harry didn't want to make life hard for his brother and sister. They were the ones who lived locally and would bear the brunt of George's temper, whereas Harry had the perfect excuse to escape to wherever the quartet was playing next.

'I still think my father would turn in his grave at the idea of people poking around the house,' George grumbled.

'Nobody will be poking around the house, Pa,' Dominic reassured him. 'They'll be following a defined visitor route. Nobody will go into areas we've roped off as private. And we've done Open Garden weekends for years without a problem; opening the house to visitors is just an extension of that.'

'The gift shop, the plant sales and the café we're going to set up in the Orangery will help to make the estate pay for itself,' Ellen added. 'We're developing an exclusive range of biscuits at the factory, based on some of the old recipes we found in the library, and we can sell all the gifts through our website as well.'

'Biscuits.' George's voice dripped with contempt.

Harry could see his sister-in-law Sally and his brother-in-law Tristan squirming, embarrassed by the escalating family row and not quite sure how to deal with Viscount Moran's uncertain temper, worried that anything they did or said would make things worse. With age, George had become more and more crusty, to the point where he was almost a caricature. One of these days he'd be in a satirical cartoon, with his mop of grey hair he couldn't be bothered to style, his jowls and his red cheeks, pointing a finger and shouting.

'Well, I don't want anything to do with it.' George swigged his brandy crossly. 'I don't see why you can't just wait for me to die before you start all this nonsense.'

'That can be arranged,' Barbara said, rolling her eyes at her husband.

George's temper flared. 'As for you, what do you care about Beauchamp? You grew up—'

Harry knew what was coming next: a potshot at his mother's background as the daughter of a local biscuit manufacturer. She was a commoner with her background in trade, not the gentry. And that in turn would escalate to comments from his mother that the Morans hadn't minded the money from Beckett's Biscuits rescuing them when George's father had drunk and gambled away the estate to near-penury, forty years before...

He stood up. 'Both of you. Please. Just *stop*,' he said quietly.

To his surprise, his parents did so.

It was a heady feeling that they were actually listening to the baby of the family for once. And maybe he'd drunk too much wine, because he found himself folding his arms and looking his father straight in the eye. 'Pa, Dom and Nell are absolutely right. This house eats money and it needs to start paying its way. You'll still have your private space and nobody's going to disturb that. We're simply letting people enjoy the garden and the artworks here, and it'll mean you won't have to sell yet another painting to pay for the next lot of repairs and work out how you're going to hide the faded patch on the walls because you can't afford to renovate the silk wall coverings.'

George stared at him in complete silence.

Warming to his theme, Harry said, 'A gift shop with plant sales and a café will create jobs and bring in visitors to help the local economy. Everyone wins. Dom, Sally, Nell and Tris all work really hard and they're doing a brilliant job. We all ought to appreciate that.'

More silence, and this time he could see that his brother and sister were squirming just as much as their partners.

He'd gone too far.

But he really wasn't going to apologise. Not this time. He hadn't said anything offensive. And he was so tired of treading on eggshells around his irascible father. Viscount Moran and his moods had dominated the family ever since Harry could remember, and it was way past time that changed. Harry was sick of having to kowtow to an entitled bully. 'Excuse me,' he said. 'I'll go and get some more water.' He picked up the jug from the centre of the table and headed for the kitchen.

Ellen followed him. 'Are you all right, Harry?'

'Yeah.' He sighed. 'Sorry, Nell. I didn't intend to stir things up. But I'm so sick of it. This is why I hardly ever come back to the abbey. I'm tired of Ma and Pa sniping at each other all the time. And I'm really tired of them treating you and Dom as if you're useless, when actually you're brilliant and without the pair of you Beauchamp Abbey would've collapsed under a pile of debt years and years ago.' He grimaced.

'In my professional life, I stand up to bullies. Especially if I see one of the older men trying to put the younger women down, or leering at them and trying to do the equivalent of the casting couch. It's absolutely *not* OK, and I'm not going to stand aside and watch it happen.' He sighed. 'I just wish I knew how to deal with Pa.'

'Just let it go,' Ellen advised. 'Pa can threaten whatever he likes, but he can't actually carry any of it out. Grandpa Beckett left the majority share in the biscuit business to me, so Pa can't sack me. The house is entailed, so Dom's the only one who can inherit it; and it'd take an Act of Parliament for Pa to make anyone other than Dom the next Viscount—which we all know isn't going to happen, because even people who've had a really good case for disinheriting their kids haven't been able to stop them inheriting the title and estate. Pa has absolutely no grounds for disinheriting Dom. He'd be laughed at if he tried.'

'I guess,' Harry said.

She hugged him. 'And ignore those stupid comments about your career. We're so proud of you.'

'Yes. Your quartet's booked up for two years in advance, which is pretty amazing,' Dominic said, walking into the kitchen, 'and what about the awards you've won? Plus whenever I play any of your recordings it takes me into another world. You're brilliant at what you do. Don't listen to Pa.'

'I was all ready to yell at him and tell him to stop being such a bully,' Harry said, 'but I stopped myself because I know I won't be the one who has to put up with the tantrums, and it isn't fair to make things worse for you. But I really, *really* hate the way he treats you all.'

'It is what it is,' Dominic said with a shrug. 'I don't think you're old enough to remember, but Grandpa Moran was even worse than Pa.'

'So why doesn't Pa think about how

Grandpa Moran made him feel, and ask himself if that's how he wants his own children to think about him?' Harry asked.

'Because I don't think he can. He's too set in his ways,' Ellen said gently. 'But we love you, Harry. And we're hugely proud of you.'

'Seconded,' Dominic said, clapping him on the shoulder.

'Though,' Ellen added, 'he might have a point about letting someone back into your life. I know you were in pieces when Rochelle... Well.' She coughed. 'But that doesn't mean it wouldn't work with anyone else.'

Oh, but it would. Harry had faced a stark choice: his marriage or his career. And he'd chosen the thing built on solid foundations. The thing where he could be himself and not think about the might-have-beens: the little boy or girl who would've been five years old now.

'Thank you for your support,' he said, 'but I don't need anyone. I'm fine.'

'We worry about you,' Ellen said.

'I'm fine. Really,' he said. 'Just sick of the parents.' He grimaced. 'They loathe each other, but they'll never get divorced. They always bang on about divorce not being the done thing—' and they'd both gone on about it most when he could've done with a bit of support, in the middle of his own divorce '—but I think we all know Ma married Pa for his title, and Pa married Ma for Grandpa Beckett's money. Divorce means she'd lose the title and he'd lose the money. So they stay together and just make each other—and everyone around them—utterly miserable.'

'Which is why we don't live here with them.' Ellen ruffled his hair. 'Living in the village means there's just enough distance between us to protect the kids. But not all marriages are like theirs, Harry. Or like yours was, sweetheart. Look at me and Dom. I'm happy with Tris.'

'And I'm happy with Sal,' Dominic said. 'I know it was hard, what happened with Rochelle, but surely it's worth trying again?'

Harry sighed. The wreckage had proved that he should never have married Rochelle in the first place. Marriage wasn't for him. Not then and not now. 'The women who want to date me nowadays don't see the real me—they see either Harry the musician in the public eye, or Harry the younger son of Viscount Moran.'

'Then you're meeting the wrong women,' Ellen said. 'Why don't you let me—?'

'Thanks for the offer, but no,' Harry cut in gently. The last thing he wanted was for his sister to start match-making, even though he respected her judgement. He didn't want to fall in love again, only for it to go wrong. He couldn't face any more ultimatums with a woman saying he had to choose between her and his music. Clearly it was greedy to want love *and* his job. But at least his job never let him down, unlike love.

Ellen took a key from her pocket. 'Here. Escape back to ours, and get some fresh air. I'll tell the parents you've got a migraine.'

'You,' Harry said, 'are the best sister ever.'

She grinned. 'I hope so. Do you really have to dash off tomorrow?'

Harry nodded. 'Sorry, I have rehearsals.'

On Thursday evening, Holly was in the middle of packing her bag for the weekend when her phone shrilled.

'Hey, Nat,' she said, answering the call.

'Holls, I'm so sorry.' Natalie sounded thoroughly miserable. 'There's been a bug going round at work and I've picked it up—I've been throwing up all day and I feel like death warmed up.'

'You poor thing,' Holly said. 'Look, I'll ring the hotel and cancel, and then I'll come round and make you something with apples and rice that you might be able to keep down.'

'No, don't come here—you might go down with this bug, too,' Natalie said. 'And don't cancel. You picked up the dresses for us yesterday, so you can still go to Bath.'

'Without you? No way!'

'It's all paid for,' Natalie said, 'and at this late notice we wouldn't get a refund. It's daft to waste the money.'

'I can try asking,' Holly said, 'or see if they can reschedule.'

'No. You go without me,' Natalie urged. 'Have a good time and take lots of pictures for me.'

It wouldn't be the same on her own, but Holly didn't want to throw her best friend's kindness back in her face. 'Only,' she said, 'on condition that we reschedule a weekend away for both of us later in the summer, and it'll be *my* treat.'

'Deal,' Natalie said. 'And this time I'll try not to pick up any horrible sicky bugs.'

'I'll bring you back a Sally Lunn on Sunday evening,' Holly promised, knowing how much Natalie enjoyed the historic Bath speciality: a teacake that was a bit like a brioche, made from a recipe dating back to Restoration times.

'Jane Austen's favourite—and mine,' Natalie said. 'And I really hope I feel better by Sunday so I can do it justice!'

* * *

On Friday, Holly caught the train to Bath after work. Breakfast the next morning was as good as Natalie had promised; and then she headed to re-acquaint herself with the Roman Baths and drool over the lead curse tablets. She took a selfie while she drank a paper cup of the slightly warm and slightly disgusting water at the baths and sent it to Natalie, and followed it up with photographs of the gorgeous Georgian houses, tour guides walking around the city dressed up as Mr Darcy, and detailed pictures of the afternoon tea at the Pump Room. She called in at the ancient shop to buy a Sally Lunn, and picked up chocolates from the artisanal maker Natalie had been raving about since their last visit, then headed back to get ready for the ball.

She really didn't want to go.

But Natalie had paid for the tickets and Holly felt it would be churlish to deny her friend a few photographs to cheer her up.

The red dress Natalie had chosen for her fitted perfectly. It had a flattering Empire line bodice, short puff sleeves, a net overskirt and a silk underskirt, and Natalie had also hired a pair of long white gloves and a small reticule to go with it. Thankfully Holly had a pair of flat black suede pumps that would work as dance shoes.

She knew from the costume events her best friend had attended in the past that she needed to put her hair up; she was used to wearing her hair tied back at the nape of her neck or in a braid for work, so it didn't take her long to put her hair up in a bun, braid a section that she could twist round the bun, and then curl the strands at the front. She added the bare minimum of make-up, then took a selfie in the full-length mirror.

She really didn't look like the scruffy archaeologist Simon had rejected; she barely recognised the woman in the photograph. So maybe tonight she could be whoever she wanted.

She sent the selfie to her best friend. 'OK?'

'More than OK. Utterly perfect,' was Natalie's verdict. 'Have fun!'

A ball wasn't Holly's idea of fun, but she duly took a taxi to the venue.

Natalie had been right to choose this dress. It made Holly feel amazing. How long had it been since she'd felt this confident in herself? She hadn't even felt confident when she'd tried on the wedding dress—which in itself should've been a sign that she had been doing the wrong thing. Maybe, she thought,

Simon's defection actually meant she'd had a lucky escape from a marriage that would eventually have made her miserable.

And she wasn't going to think of her ex any more. She was going to enjoy the evening. She'd listen to good music, eat good food, and soak up the history.

The manor house was utterly gorgeous— built from mellow golden stone in the traditional Elizabethan 'E' shape, with pointed gables, ornate chimney stacks and stone mullioned windows. She smiled as she paid the driver and crunched along the gravel path to the front door; Nat was definitely right about her loving the house.

Inside was even better. There was a grand entrance hall and a library with an elaborate plaster ceiling, tall bookcases and oak panelling around huge windows. Better still was the first-floor gallery, which actually stretched the whole length of the house, and just off it was the ballroom where Regency dancing was already taking place. Holly took a few shots for Natalie, knowing her friend would love seeing all the costumes, then went through to the gallery and looked out into the gardens. Below was a perfect knot garden that echoed the design of the ceiling in the library; the framework of box hedge was

filled in with lavender, rosemary and mar-
joram, with strategically placed alliums and
roses. On a warm late spring evening like
this, it would smell heavenly.

Behind the knot garden were lawns that
sloped down to the lake, and she could see
a bandstand in the middle with a small boat
tied up just behind it. The string quartet was
already in place; and hadn't Natalie suggested
that she could just sit outside and listen to the
music with a glass of Pimm's? Better that
than being a wallflower in the ballroom,
Holly thought, and headed out to listen to
the music.

CHAPTER TWO

HARRY SETTLED INTO his chair on the bandstand; he'd checked the set-up beforehand, making sure there were four armless chairs and good overhead lighting for the musicians, and they'd all come across on the lake on the flat-bottomed motor launch. Thankfully it was warm enough to play outside without risking damage to their instruments; and actually he loved the idea of playing in the middle of a lake.

They'd been booked to play for two hours, and between them they'd come up with a mixture of classical music and film tunes that their audience should enjoy. Thankfully none of the others in the quartet was a music snob and they enjoyed playing the crowd-pleasers as much as he did, from Pachelbel to Bach to Mozart.

'I know we're already playing "The Swan",' Lucy, the quartet's viola player, said, 'but, since people have seen us get over here on a boat shaped like a swan, I think we ought to do "Dance of the Little Swans" as well.'

'Agreed,' Drew and Stella, the quartet's violinists, said.

'Or,' Harry suggested, 'a bit of T-Rex. "Ride a White Swan".' He plucked a couple of bars to illustrate his point. 'Or there's—'

'None of your experimental stuff tonight,' Lucy cut in with a grin, clearly having a good idea what he was going to suggest next. 'We're only playing music people know well. Traditional stuff.'

'"Dance of the Little Swans" it is,' Harry capitulated. 'Let's do that first.' The venue was beautiful and the event tonight made him think of all the things his family could do with Beauchamp Abbey, if his father wasn't so difficult. Though he shoved the thought away. Tonight wasn't about Viscount Moran. Harry was just going to enjoy the gorgeous late spring evening, and the joy of playing music he adored in such a fabulous setting.

They began with the Tchaikovsky, and segued into Harry's arrangement of Fauré's 'Sicilienne' before playing the first of the show tunes. People came to sit at the edge of the lake for a while, then drifted off again to go back for the dancing, while others took a break from the dancing and came to enjoy the quartet.

As the sun slowly went down, the sky turning amazing colours that were reflected in the lake, their audience grew smaller; but Harry noticed one woman in a red dress who seemed to be there for the entire performance. Usually people came to a ball in couples or in groups; he wondered why she was sitting alone. And it distracted him to the point where he nearly missed a note; cross with himself, he refocused and tried not to look at her.

But, despite his best efforts, something about the woman in red drew him. To the point where the only way he could concentrate was to promise himself that, as soon as he was back on dry land, he'd go in search of her and say hello.

Holly adored the music that the string quartet was playing. There was some really clever adaptation of music from shows and pieces that were usually performed by larger orchestral groups; she really loved Gershwin's 'Summertime', with the focus on the solo cello, and Bach's 'Air on a G String'. She could've listened to them play all night. Even though the sun had set and it was starting to get chilly, she really didn't want to go back inside the hall for the dancing.

She sat at the water's edge until the swan-shaped motor launch brought the quartet back to shore, then decided to go inside for just long enough to take a couple of pictures for Natalie before heading back to her hotel in the centre of Bath. She was about to haul herself to her feet when a man sat down beside her on the bank. 'Hello.'

He was absolutely gorgeous, with dark hair and midnight-blue eyes; and he was dressed like a Regency buck in white pantaloons, a white linen shirt with a fancy cravat, a cream silk waistcoat and a navy tailcoat. Holly was shocked to find that it was suddenly hard to breathe. She didn't react to men like this. Ever. She hadn't even felt like this when she'd met Simon. Oh, for pity's sake, what was wrong with her? She just about managed to reply with a shy, 'Hello.'

'I noticed you sitting here earlier. Would you mind if I joined you?'

Help. When was the last time anyone had chatted her up? Simon, eight years ago—and look how badly that had turned out. Holly was about to make a flimsy excuse to leave, but she could hear her best friend's voice in her head: *The best way to get over someone is to have a mad fling...*

She had no intention of doing that, but it wouldn't kill her to have a conversation with a handsome stranger. Though it would help if she didn't look at him, because those gorgeous blue eyes took her breath away. 'Sure.'

'Are you all right?'

'Yes. Why do you ask?'

'It's getting chillier out here, the music has stopped, and there's dancing inside,' he said.

'Dancing isn't really my thing,' she admitted.

'Which rather begs the question why you came to a ball.' Though he didn't look snooty. He looked intrigued. Interested. As if he wanted to know more about her.

'My best friend organised the tickets—except she went down with a tummy bug, and persuaded me to come anyway.'

'So you're here alone?' He grimaced. 'Sorry. That sounded a bit creepy, which really wasn't my intention.'

'It's fine.' Though she appreciated the fact he was sensitive. 'I was about to call a taxi back to my hotel.'

'Have you eaten tonight?' he asked.

'No,' she admitted.

'Neither have I. Come and have something

at the buffet with me, and I'll give you a lift back into the city afterwards,' he invited. 'As long as you don't mind sitting in the front of the car with me—I'm afraid my cello takes up the entire back seat.'

Then Holly realised who he was. 'You were playing in the bandstand earlier.'

He inclined his head. 'The ball was organised by a close friend of Lucy, our viola player, so we agreed to play here tonight. Actually, it was fun—I haven't played in the middle of a lake before, and it's definitely the first time I've gone anywhere by swan.'

'I really enjoyed the music,' she said, and then was cross with herself for sounding so star-struck and gauche.

He smiled. 'I rather hoped that was why you were sitting there all evening.'

He'd noticed that? Then again, there weren't many women here wearing dresses the same colour as hers. Most were wearing cream or navy. 'Natalie, my best friend, said she thought I'd end up out here listening to the music rather than dancing.' She shivered, suddenly aware of the cold.

He noticed, because he shrugged off his tailcoat and placed it around her shoulders.

'Thank you. That's very gallant—and quite befitting a Regency gentleman,' she said.

'I'm Harry,' he said, holding his hand out to shake hers. 'Nice to meet you.'

'Holly. Often as prickly as my name,' she said. And how weird it was that her skin tingled when she took his hand to shake it. She'd never experienced that before either.

He grinned. 'I must remember that when I get accused of being overly pushy. Harry by name, harry by nature.'

Maybe it was a warning; but she instinctively liked him and he didn't strike her as being the difficult type. Then again, her intuition had been way off beam with Simon. Could she trust her intuition any more? On the other hand, he was a stranger. She could be whoever she wanted tonight: the woman in a red dress who stood out from the crowd.

Her confidence back, she pushed her doubts aside and walked back to the house with him. 'The music was so wonderful, I assume you've played together for some time.'

'Professionally, for about six years,' he said. 'We went to the same college and all hit it off, so it made sense to work together afterwards.'

'Six years? Are you quite well known, then?' The awkwardness came back. 'I apologise for not recognising you.'

'I'm not quite on the same level as Jacqueline du Pré or Steven Isserlis,' he said with a smile.

Meaning that he was actually rather well known but was modest about it, Holly thought. She liked the way he was so matter-of-fact.

'I don't actually care whether people recognise me or not, as long I get to play. The music is what really matters,' he said.

'Do what you love and love what you do,' she mused. 'My grandfather was fond of saying that.'

'Your grandfather was a wise man,' he said.

'Very,' she agreed.

She gave the tailcoat back to Harry as soon as they reached the house, then went in to the buffet with him. They watched the dancers while they ate.

'Are you sure I can't tempt you?' he asked, gesturing to the dance floor.

'I'm very sure,' she said with a smile, 'unless you're seriously good at Regency dancing and can teach me all the steps in about three seconds flat.'

'Or we could do the alternative—there's another room for those who enjoy dressing up in all the Regency finery but would rather stick to more modern dancing. One dance, and then I'll take you back to your hotel?' he suggested.

The sensible thing would be to say no, and get the taxi.

But something in his blue, blue eyes drew her.

'One dance,' Holly said. 'Though you'll still need to show me the steps.'

Simon had never really been into dancing, so she'd never actually learned how to do ballroom dancing—just the slightly awkward shuffle that most students did at discos and formal balls. She'd always thought that she had two left feet. But dancing with Harry the cellist was something else entirely. Especially because the next dance was a waltz, and Harry dipped and swayed and spun her, guiding her movements so she felt as if she was gliding on air, not putting a single foot wrong.

He swept her off her feet to the point where one dance led to two, then three.

And when the music changed from a formal ballroom dance to a soft, slow dance, Harry drew her closer and she found her arms were wrapped around him. They were so close together that she could feel his heart beating, strong and slightly fast—just like her own.

Dancing cheek to cheek.

So this was what it felt like.

Not the awkward and slightly embarrassing shuffle of her student years, but something that made her feel breathless and dizzy. The feeling increased as she realised that Harry had moved his head so that his lips were just touching the corner of her mouth. All she had to do was to move her head a tiny fraction and his lips would be against hers.

Could she?

Should she?

Her heart rate kicked up a notch as she shifted a tiny, tiny fraction. Suddenly the music and everything else around her vanished: all she was aware of was Harry, and the way he made her feel. Her lips touched his, and his arms tightened round her. He brushed his mouth against hers, almost as if asking permission, and then she kissed him lightly in response. And then they were really kissing, clinging to each other as if they were drowning.

When was the last time she'd been kissed like this, making her feel as if she were burning up from the inside out? She couldn't remember. All she could focus on was the feeling, right here, right now.

He broke the kiss and his gaze held hers. 'Shall we get out of here?'

Holly was shocked to realise that she'd completely blanked out her surroundings. She'd just let a total stranger sweep her off her feet and kiss her stupid in the middle of a crowded ballroom. This wasn't what she did. She was sensible Holly Weston, usually found in a lecture theatre or in a trench somewhere, wearing jeans and a sensible long-sleeved shirt and a hat to protect her from the sun and insects. The woman wearing a red Regency dress, dancing in a ballroom, felt like a completely different person.

Out of here, he'd suggested. She nodded, and he took her hand and led her out of the hall. They stopped to collect his cello, and Holly thought that her common sense was starting to come back—but then they got to his car and he kissed her again, and her common sense vanished once more at the speed of light.

He drove them back to Bath. Then, as they reached the outskirts of the city, he said, 'I can drop you at your hotel now. Or perhaps you'd like to come back to where I'm staying and have a drink with me?'

Holly opened her mouth, intending to tell him that dropping her by the train station was just fine, thank you—but her libido had clearly overpowered her common sense, because she found herself saying, 'I'd love to come back for a drink. Thank you.'

Was she *crazy*?

She didn't know this man at all.

OK, so he played the cello beautifully—but he was still a stranger, and they hadn't even swapped surnames. This was real life, where you didn't go off with someone you didn't know, no matter how amazing his kisses were or how brilliantly he played the cello. What on earth was she doing?

Then he pulled up outside a sweeping Georgian terrace, a building she recognised as one of Bath's landmarks.

'You're staying *here*?' She blinked in surprise. 'Are you telling me you own a flat in this building?'

'No, I'm borrowing it. It belongs to an old friend. Ferdy lives in London, but he spends most of his weekends here. As he's not here this particular weekend, he lent me the key to his *pied-à-terre*,' Harry said with a smile.

Clearly Harry the cellist was very well connected. She hadn't registered it before that moment, but his car was an expensive saloon. Top of the range. And a flat in this building would be eye-wateringly expensive for a main home, let alone a second. So either Harry was a lot more famous than he admitted to being, or he came from a really wealthy background. In both cases, she didn't measure up.

Par for the course.

She really ought to make an excuse and go back to her hotel. Except it would be rude, given that she'd already accepted his invitation. And he'd been so nice. And, actually, she wanted to spend more time with him.

'Come in,' he said, and retrieved his cello from the back of the car.

Once he'd unlocked the front door, he ushered her inside and tapped in the code to switch off the alarm.

'This is amazing,' she said, taking in the plasterwork on the ceiling, the deep cream-coloured walls and the elaborate doorframes. 'The perfect Georgian flat.' And how appropriate that both she and Harry were dressed in Georgian finery.

'Let me give you the grand tour,' Harry said. 'This is the sitting room.'

It had a high ceiling with a very elegant chandelier; the walls were painted a deep mustard colour and there were floor-to-ceiling sash windows dressed with dark blue velvet curtains, complementing the deep mustard velvet sofas. The black-leaded fireplace had deep blue tiles and a white marble surround, and the stripped wood floor had a rug in the centre in tones of blue and mustard. The whole thing felt distinctly Georgian; even the paintings looked appropriate to the era, with large portraits of women and children in Georgian clothing.

'Are they family portraits?' she asked.

'Probably. Knowing Ferdy, he most likely borrowed them from his gran,' Harry said.

She and Harry were from very different worlds; in hers, there might be a few photographs of great-great-grandparents if you were lucky, but actual painted portraits? She'd never met anyone like that.

He took off his jacket and laid it across the back of one of the sofas, then set his cello case down safely on the floor before ushering her to the next doorway. 'I think you can work this one out for yourself,' he said, gesturing to the kitchen-diner. Like the sitting room, the room had a stripped wooden floor, though the walls here were painted duck-egg blue. There were white painted cabinets, which she assumed also hid the fridge and freezer, and a discreet state-of-the-art cooker. At one end of the room there was a table with six chairs and a dresser with antique china plates, cups and saucers on display. More of his friend's family heirlooms? she wondered.

'Bedroom,' Harry said, gesturing to the one closed door. 'And the bathroom.'

The claw-footed free-standing bath was perfect, its outside a soft dove grey that toned with the darker grey walls and the white marble fireplace.

He ushered her back to the kitchen. 'Can I offer you coffee, tea or champagne?'

'Actually, a cup of tea would be really lovely, please,' she said.

He smiled at her, filled the kettle, and rummaged in the cupboard. 'Do you prefer builder's tea, Earl Grey, green tea, or something that looks like pot-pourri?' he asked.

'Builder's tea is perfect, thank you,' she said.

'I'll let you add your own milk,' he said. 'Um—would you mind if the milk was straight from the carton, or shall I try and find the milk jug?'

'Straight from the carton is fine,' she said. She was more used to drinking from a chipped mug balanced on the edge of a trench or among the papers on her desk, rather than from porcelain, and with the tea made from a tea-bag rather than loose leaves in a matching porcelain pot with what looked like a solid silver strainer.

'OK. Sugar?'

'No, thanks.'

He let the tea brew, then poured two cups and handed her the carton of milk. 'To an unexpected evening,' he said, raising his tea cup in a toast.

'An unexpected evening,' she echoed, doing the same—no way would she risk chinking her cup against his and chipping it.

'Shall we go through to the sitting room?'

She followed him through, and couldn't resist looking out of the window. Even though it was dark, the street lights outside showed her how lovely the view must be in daylight.

'Ferdy gets a view of the sunset from here. It's gorgeous.' He paused. 'Holly. Just so you know, I never invite people back to wherever I'm staying, especially when I've only just met them. It's just...' He shook his head. 'I don't know. There's something about you.'

'I don't ever go off with total strangers either,' she said. 'But tonight...' It was the same for her. An instant connection she'd felt between them. Something strange and new and irresistible. Possibly much too soon, given that she'd only been officially single for three weeks; then again, if she looked back she could see the cracks in her relationship even before Simon's secondment to New York, and apart from that brief weekend she hadn't seen him for six months.

'Can I ask you something pushy?' she asked.

'Sure,' he said.

'Could I ask you to play something for me?'

'Of course.' He took the cello from its case, then checked the tuning and looked at her. 'What would you like me to play?'

'Anything you like. Your favourite piece,' she suggested.

'That rather changes with my mood,' he said.

'OK. Your favourite piece right now,' she said.

He grinned. 'Do you mind something really flashy and showy-offy?'

'Bring it on,' she said.

He proceeded to play something that was the equivalent of cello pyrotechnics; she recognised the tune but couldn't name it.

'That was amazing,' she said.

'Paganini's "Caprice No. 24"—it's a lot of fun to play,' he said. 'Given that you sat through our entire set, I assume you like classical music?'

'Yes, but I don't hear much live,' she said. 'I've been to a couple of Proms, but that's about it. This is a huge treat.'

He inclined his head in acknowledgement, and played something much slower for her.

'I really like that,' she said. 'What is it?'

'"Hushabye Mountain", from *Chitty Chitty Bang Bang*,' he said. 'It's a gorgeous arrangement.'

He followed up with a song she recognised as an eighties classic: 'Don't You Forget About Me'.

Harry was the least forgettable man she'd ever met. Not that she was gauche enough to say so. 'That was great, too,' she said when he'd finished.

He smiled and put his cello away. 'My turn to be pushy. Will you dance with me again?' he asked.

She nodded, and he connected his phone to Ferdy's audio system; then he dimmed the lights as soft music flooded into the room, and placed both of their cups on the low coffee table.

Again, he made her feel as if she was dancing on air. And this time, when they kissed, there was nothing to make her hold back.

'Holly.' His eyes were almost black in the low light. 'Stay with me tonight.'

A night with no strings. A night of pure pleasure. A bubble of time outside her real life. She could be sensible and call a taxi

back to her hotel—or she could follow her
impulses for once.

But she still had enough common sense to
check something, first. Because she had no
intention of hurting someone else, the way
Simon had hurt her. 'There's no one who
could be hurt by this? You're single?'

'I'm single,' he confirmed.

'Then, yes, I'll stay,' she said.

'Good,' he said, and led her out of the living room. Still holding her hand, he opened
the door to the bedroom. The walls were
painted deep red, but the thing that really
drew her eye was the bed: a half-tester in
dark wood with deep red and gold hangings.
Her mouth went dry.

Then he lifted her up and carried her across
the threshold, for all the world as if she really
was a demure Regency maiden.

'Holly,' he whispered, setting her down on
her feet. 'Are you quite sure about this? Because you can change your mind and it will
be OK. I can drive you back to your hotel.'

The sensible thing to do would be to accept
his offer of a lift home.

But right now she didn't feel very sensible.
Right now, she could see the whole point of
Natalie's view that the best way to get over
someone was to have a fling with someone

else. No strings, no promises—and nobody to get hurt, because she and Harry were both single.

'I'm sure,' she whispered back, wrapped her arms round his neck, and kissed him.

The next morning, Holly woke to the scent of coffee. Sunday morning. The memories of the previous night rushed through her head.

Oh, help. How did you behave the morning after a mad fling?

She could get dressed, creep along the hallway to grab her bag from where she'd left it… In the kitchen, where from the smell of coffee in the air she presumed that Harry was busy. Not to mention that this was an old building and, despite modernisation work, the floorboards probably creaked. Creeping out clearly wasn't an option.

Get dressed and brazen it out, pretending that she did this sort of thing all the time? Again, that wasn't an option, because she'd admitted to him the previous night that she didn't usually do this sort of thing.

Before she could worry about the situation any more, Harry leaned round the door. 'Good morning.'

'Good morning.' She gave him an awkward smile. He was wearing jeans and a T-shirt and his hair was damp, so clearly he'd already showered and dressed.

'I have coffee brewing and I just picked up some freshly baked croissants from the deli round the corner. Help yourself to anything you need in the bathroom. Ferdy keeps a bath robe for guests on the back of the bathroom door, if you need it.'

'Thank you.' So at least she wouldn't need to have breakfast in her Regency dress and risk spilling something on it and wrecking it before it went back to the hire place.

'And there's a spare toothbrush in the bathroom cabinet,' he added.

Harry's friend Ferdy kept his bathroom very well appointed, and Holly managed to shower without getting her hair wet. Wearing the borrowed bath robe, she padded barefoot into the kitchen.

'Help yourself to milk and sugar,' Harry said, pouring coffee into a mug and putting it in front of her.

He'd laid the table with a jug of freshly squeezed orange juice, a bowl of fresh strawberries, yoghurt, butter and jam, as well as a large glass jar of granola; he took the still-warm croissants from a paper bag and put them on a plate.

'This is really lovely,' she said shyly. 'Thank you.'

'My pleasure.' He smiled at her. 'I'm guessing right now that you feel as weird as I do.'

She nodded.

'I don't make a habit of this,' he said. 'But I don't regret last night.'

Neither, she discovered, did she. 'Snap.'

'Then let's just ignore the awkwardness,' he said. 'Are you busy today?'

'I'm due back in London this evening,' she said.

'So theoretically we could have lunch together, and maybe do something touristy? There's an amazing park not far from here, or we could follow in Jane Austen's footsteps and walk through Sydney Gardens to the canal.'

Meaning that last night might not be just a one-off?

Though Harry was a professional musician. He probably toured a lot. They might live hundreds of miles apart, and seeing each other could be difficult.

Then again, there was that connection between them. Maybe they should give it a chance and see where it took them. He'd told her last night that he was single; and, thanks to her broken engagement, so was she. There was no reason why they couldn't spend today together and see what happened.

'I'd like that,' she said. 'Though I really need to go back to my hotel and change first.'

'Of course. I can give you a lift, when you're ready to go,' he said.

'No, it's fine. I don't mind walking,' she said. 'So are you staying in Bath for a few days?'

'Sadly not. I'm driving to Birmingham tonight,' he said, 'because I'm recording tomorrow.'

Whereas she would going back to mark dissertations and be on hand to calm her students down before their exams. Their lives were very different. 'Uh-huh.'

'So do you know Bath well?' he asked.

She nodded. 'My best friend is a huge Jane Austen fan.'

'Have you been to the Roman Baths?' he asked.

'Yes,' she said, not wanting to admit that she'd also done some work on the site because it sounded a bit precious. 'And I've taken the waters.'

'They're absolutely vile. Or maybe I'm biased because the only time I ever tasted them I had a hangover, and Ferdy insisted on using the Bath cure.'

'Did it work?'

'No.' He grimaced, and then gave her a boyish grin that put the most appealing crinkles at the corners of his eyes. 'Though I'm pretty sure that Bath water tastes like bathwater, and Ferdy only told me it was a hangover cure so he could see my face when I tried it.'

She grinned back, enjoying the pun. Not only was she attracted to Harry the cellist physically, she *liked* him. And that ridiculous pun made her relax with him enough to really enjoy breakfast and just chat with him.

He insisted on clearing away while she changed back into her Regency dress.

'Are you quite sure I can't just drop you at your hotel?' he asked.

'Quite sure,' she said. 'I'll see you in an hour, outside the Pump Room.'

'Let's swap phone numbers in case either of us gets held up,' he suggested.

She took her phone from her bag, but it refused to switch on. She winced. 'Sorry, I'm utterly hopeless with my phone. It's out of charge—*again*.' She gave him her number and he tapped it into his own phone.

'See you in an hour,' he said, and kissed her at the door.

Back at the hotel, Holly put her phone on

charge, and it started to beep with incoming texts. Most of them were from Natalie. Holly quickly texted her back.

Sorry, my phone went flat. Hope you're feeling better. I took your advice!!! Tell you more later. Love you. x

She sent a couple of the photographs she'd taken the previous evening, then changed into her normal clothes, packed, checked out, and left her luggage with the hotel's concierge to collect before she had to catch her train.

While she was walking down the High Street on the way to the Pump Room, she saw a sun hat blowing into the road, and seconds later a small child darted in front of her after it. The little boy's mum was frantically trying to find the brake on the baby's pram and screaming out to her son to leave the hat and come back.

There was a car zooming down the road, and the driver clearly hadn't seen the child because he wasn't braking.

Acting purely on instinct, and because she was the nearest person to the little boy, Holly stepped into the road to grab him. She heard the screech of brakes, and everything seemed to happen in slow motion. Grabbing the child and pulling him out of danger. The car, moving closer and closer. The thud of the impact as the car hit her.

And then everything went black.

Harry glanced at his watch, frowning. They'd agreed to meet in an hour and he'd been a couple of minutes early. Maybe Holly had been held up. He'd give her a few minutes. From his spot outside the Pump Room he could see most of the area outside the cathedral door to his right, and then across part of the narrow street to his left, so whichever way she came from he'd see her quickly.

It was a gorgeous bright sunny day and he was looking forward to getting to know his mysterious lady in red a little bit better. He couldn't remember the last time he'd really clicked with someone like this; despite his usual reluctance to get involved, he found himself hoping that this might turn into more than just a weekend thing. Holly was very, very different from Rochelle. In fact, she was different from all the women he'd dated; he hadn't told her anything more than his first name, so refreshingly she hadn't seen him either as someone in the public eye or as the youngest son of Viscount Moran. She'd just seen him as one of the musicians at the ball.

An equal. And definitely not a means to financial security.

He was dimly aware of the sound of a siren somewhere beyond the cathedral, but didn't take much notice of it.

There was still no sign of Holly.

Harry waited for another half an hour.

OK, so he didn't actually know her very well, but he was pretty sure she wasn't the type of woman who would ghost someone. Maybe something had happened to hold her up. And, because her phone had died, she didn't have his number; so obviously he'd have to be the one to call her to see if she was OK.

One ring, two, three—

'Hello?'

That definitely wasn't Holly's voice; it was male and had a strong Glaswegian accent.

'I must have the wrong number. Sorry to have disturbed you,' Harry said, cut the connection, and tried again.

The phone rang twice before the Glaswegian man answered again.

'I'm sorry. I'm trying to get in touch with Holly.'

'I don't know anyone called Holly, pal,' the stranger said.

'This is the number she gave me this morning.' Harry had typed it in as she'd said it. 'Her phone had died so she gave me her number.'

The Scotsman laughed. 'It sounds as if she made it up, pal, and you're out of luck.'

'I guess. Sorry for bothering you.'

'No bother, pal. I'm sorry your girl let you down.'

Harry ended the call, flooded with disappointment and feeling thoroughly rejected. He'd never been ghosted before, and it made him feel as if he was worthless. Just like his dad always made him feel whenever George spoke about Harry's career.

Holly had been at pains last night to check that he was single and nobody could be hurt by them getting together; maybe it had been a warning sign that it hadn't been the case for her. He didn't think she seemed to be the cheating type, but then again it was now forty minutes since they'd been supposed to meet here, she hadn't shown up and the phone number she'd given him had turned out to be not hers.

No wonder she'd refused to let him drop her back at her hotel. Clearly she'd had no intention of actually meeting him.

He gritted his teeth. What an idiot he'd been. OK. He'd deal with his feelings the same way he always did—playing certain pieces of music to burn out the anger and disappointment—and then he'd drive to Birmingham now and start rehearsing. Last night had been a one-off, a bubble in time. His path was unlikely to cross hers again, and it was pointless trying to find her. Holly might not even have been her real name.

Holly. Often as prickly as my name.

She hadn't been prickly with him. She'd been warm and sweet and funny, and he'd really, really liked her.

Just a pity she clearly hadn't felt the same way about him.

And it would teach him not to give in to ridiculous impulses in future. He should've learned from his time with Rochelle that relationships weren't for him.

CHAPTER THREE

'Hɪ, ᴛʜᴇʀᴇ. Hᴏw are you feeling?' a voice asked.

Sore, tired, and with a massive headache. Where on earth was she? Why was she in bed? The last thing she could remember...

...was a complete and utter blank.

'Where am I?' Holly asked, opening her eyes and wincing at the brightness of the light.

'Hospital.'

She'd already worked that one out herself from the nurse's uniform, but it wasn't fair to be rude to the woman. 'Which hospital?'

'Bath.'

'Why?' Double why: why was she in hospital, and why was she in Bath?

'Don't you remember?' the nurse asked.

'No.' And there was something important she needed to do, but she had no idea what it was.

'Can you remember your name?' the nurse asked gently.

'Yes, of course. It's...' She scrabbled in her

memory to find her name and drew a blank. Panic flooded through her. 'I… I don't know. Why don't I know my name?'

'Try not to worry,' the nurse said. 'You've been in an accident, and you hit your head. An ambulance brought you here.'

'Accident?' She didn't remember any accident.

And she didn't know her name.

'My phone. That will tell me who I am. If it's actually charged.' She remembered that. Everyone always nagged her about the fact she was terrible about keeping her phone charged. And that scared her even more. 'How do I know I'm hopeless about remembering to charge my phone, if I don't even know my own name?' What else wasn't she remembering? Would it all come back? Or did it mean that the accident—the one she didn't remember—had caused serious damage to her brain and her life would be completely changed?

'After a head injury, sometimes people have something called retrograde amnesia. The way memory is stored means you might not remember things that happened just before the accident, or even a couple of days before, but you can remember things from longer ago,' the nurse explained.

'So how come I can't remember my name?' Holly asked. 'Because my name has always been the same.' At least, she *thought* it had. But right now she couldn't be sure of anything and it felt as if she was teetering on a narrow path up a high cliff, the ground crumbling a little more beneath her with every step.

'Try not to worry too much. Memory can be a funny thing. We don't completely understand how it works,' the nurse said. She found Holly's phone and handed it to her.

'I'm sure I can't be on my own in Bath,' Holly said. 'I don't remember planning to come here in the first place, but if I'm here on holiday then I'm sure I'd be with my mum or my best friend.'

'There was nobody with you. The person who called the ambulance was the mum of the child you saved.'

'I saved a child?' She didn't remember that either.

The nurse nodded. 'A little boy. You got him out of the way of a car.'

So why hadn't someone been with her? She didn't understand—and her head hurt when she tried to think.

Her phone was charged, to her relief. But there were no notifications on the lock screen about missed calls or new text messages. If she'd been meeting her mum or her best friend and not turned up, they would've kept calling and texting her until they got an answer.

She didn't have any explanation, and it scared her even more.

What was her passcode?

She didn't know that either, Biting her lip, she looked at the nurse. 'I can't remember the code for my phone.'

'It might come back to you later,' the nurse said. 'But maybe you filled in the information on the medical emergency tab.'

Holly couldn't remember doing that either. Or how to access it. 'I'm sorry, could you help me, please?' she asked, trying to stem the growing panic.

'Of course.' The nurse took her phone and then read out loud, '"Holly Weston".'

Holly. She tested the name in her head. It felt right.

'It says you have no medical conditions,' the nurse said, handing the phone back to her, 'but it seems you're allergic to penicillin.'

Simon had made her put that in, for when she was on a dig. Just in case something happened.

Thank you, Simon, she thought gratefully, thinking of her fiancé.

Except Simon's name wasn't listed under

the emergency contacts. Just her mum and her dad.

Memories came leaking back. Simon video-calling her to say he couldn't go through with the wedding. That he'd fallen in love with his colleague Fenella and she was pregnant…

And the misery felt almost as sharp as it had been the first time round.

OK. Separate issue, she told herself. That wasn't going to change. Deal with the important stuff—the urgent stuff—first. Why was she here?

'What day is it?' she asked.

'It's Sunday.'

Today and yesterday were both a complete blank, and the entire week before was spotty. She had no idea where she'd been staying or who she'd come here with or why she was even in Bath in the first place.

'Can I ring someone for you?' the nurse asked.

'Can I call my mum?' Holly asked.

'Yes.'

'Thank you.' Holly took a deep breath. 'Can I go home?'

'I can't discharge you,' the nurse said. 'You need to see one of the doctors.'

'But I feel absolutely fine,' Holly fibbed.

There was an enormous gap in her memory that she'd try to fill in later, a headache that could be sorted with painkillers—and she'd ignore the soreness and tiredness because they'd go eventually. 'Can I see a doctor, please?'

The nurse narrowed her eyes, but said, 'I'll go and see if I can find a doctor.'

'Mum, there's been an accident,' Holly said when her mother answered. 'I'm all right, but I'm in hospital. In Bath. Apparently I saved a child from being hit by a car, but I don't remember anything.'

'Oh, my God. I'm on my way now,' Holly's mum said.

'You don't have to come,' Holly lied, really wanting to see her mum; and how ridiculous was it that tears were leaking down her face? This wasn't her. She was cool, calm, efficient Holly Weston. Nothing fazed her, which was why her colleagues had nicknamed her 'Lara Croft'.

And that was another bit of memory back. Please, please let the rest of it return, too.

'You're in hospital, love. Of course I'm coming,' Ginny Weston said.

'I don't even know if they're going to let me out today.'

'Then I'll find a hotel and I'll stay nearby

until they do,' Ginny said firmly. 'Love you, Holls. I'll be there soon.'

'Love you, Mum. And thank you.'

By the time she'd finished the call and scrubbed the tears from her face, the nurse had come back with a doctor.

'I'm Anya Singh, consultant in the emergency department,' the doctor introduced herself. 'Janet here tells me you can't remember anything from this morning.'

'I can't remember anything from the entire weekend,' Holly admitted.

'OK. Well, you dashed out in front of a car and saved a little boy from being harmed,' Anya said. 'The car hit you, you hit your head, and you've been unconscious for a while. Can I do some tests?'

'If it means I can go home, you can do anything you like,' Holly said.

Anya grinned. 'That's what I like. Cooperative patients.'

Holly submitted to a barrage of tests.

'Now can I go home?' she asked, when they were all done.

'No,' Anya said. 'I want you kept in for observation. And I'm sending you for a CT scan just to check there isn't any brain injury we haven't picked up.'

'I'm fine. Isn't some memory loss after an accident like this normal?'

'Often it's just a couple of minutes before the moment of impact,' Anya said. 'And you were unconscious for long enough for me to worry that something might be brewing. I want you here in case it is.'

'If the scan's OK, can I go home?'

'Once I'm happy that you're not going to develop a brain injury, *then* you can go home,' Anya said firmly. 'Provided you have someone to keep an eye on you for at least the first twenty-four hours after we discharge you, and you need to rest.'

Holly thought about it. 'I live on my own.' At least, she assumed she did. 'But my mum will make me stay with her.'

'Good. I'll get that scan organised,' Anya said, and patted her hand. 'Don't be stubborn. Tell us if you're hurting anywhere. Otherwise you'll be staying here for a week.'

Holly grinned, liking the doctor's sense of humour. 'Got it.'

Three days later, Holly was back in London under her mother's watchful eye, and Natalie had called round to visit.

'I feel so guilty,' Natalie said. 'If I hadn't

made you go to Bath on your own, it wouldn't have happened.'

'You'll drive yourself crazy, thinking like that. I'm fine. No harm done,' Holly said. Just her lost memory; bits of the week before had come back, but the weekend remained a stubborn blank.

'So the accident means you didn't meet your fling,' Natalie said.

Holly frowned. 'What fling?'

Natalie showed Holly the text she'd sent. 'If you really *did* take my advice, that means you had a fling.'

'If I didn't turn up to meet this guy,' Holly pointed out, 'surely he would have called me?'

'Maybe he thought you deliberately stood him up,' Natalie countered. 'Why don't you ring him?'

'And say what? "Sorry I didn't turn up, but I got hit by a car, and I don't remember a thing about you"?' Holly asked wryly. 'I'm sure he'd be thrilled to find out he was so unmemorable. Not that he exists. I was probably just teasing you.'

'I don't think you were. Give me your phone.' Natalie checked the contact list. 'Oh,' she said, sounding disappointed. 'I know everyone in your phone list.'

'They're all either related to me, work with me or are very old friends,' Holly pointed out.

'You could just drop them all a text and ask if they accompanied you to Bath.'

'No,' Holly said firmly. 'Besides, if I'd agreed to meet anyone on that list, they would already have called me to see if I was OK.' She was solid, safe and reliable; or, from Simon's point of view, boring and unable to make his heart beat fast enough. The irony didn't escape her that his job—accountancy—was notorious for being boring.

'So no leads there to your mystery man, then,' Natalie said.

Holly shrugged. 'As I said, I was probably teasing you.'

'I'm not so sure. You didn't text me until Sunday morning—so my theory is you didn't actually go back to the hotel on Saturday night. You went somewhere with your fling.' Natalie flicked into the photographs. 'Oh. No selfies. At least, none of you with the mystery man.'

'I honestly think I must've been teasing. I'm too sensible to do anything else.' And too plain and ordinary for a stranger to sweep her off her feet.

'Maybe you're right.' Natalie looked disappointed. 'I'm still worried about you, though. You spent two days in hospital, and now you're staying with your mum under hospital orders.'

'It's only a precaution. I'm absolutely fine. I simply have a bit of a gap in my memory.' Holly said. 'If I'd missed anything urgent, someone would've reminded me about it by now.' She shrugged again. 'I guess we'll just have to put the last few days down as being my "lost weekend".'

'That's the fourth take you've messed up, Harry.' Lucy handed him a mug of coffee. 'Chug this down. It might wake you up a bit so you start playing the right notes in the right order.'

'Sorry.' Harry grimaced. 'I don't know why I'm playing so badly today.'

'You've had a really amazing job offer and you don't know how to tell us that we need to find another cellist to replace you?' she suggested.

'No.'

'What, then?' she asked. 'You haven't been the same since we played on that lake outside Bath.'

No. Because he couldn't quite get Holly out of his head. Even though he knew it was ridiculous, because she'd stood him up and clearly wasn't interested.

'Harry—have you fallen for someone?'

'That's a bit out of left field,' he said, horrified that he was so transparent.

'So *that's* it. Spill.'

He sighed. Lucy had been one of his best friends for a decade and she knew him too well. If he didn't tell her, she'd nag until he did, so it was easier to give in. 'And it's ridiculous,' he finished. 'She obviously didn't want to see me again or she wouldn't have given me the wrong number.'

'Her battery was flat. Maybe the problem was with your typing,' Lucy pointed out.

'I don't think so.' He gave her a speaking look. 'If I can sight-read a complex score, then surely I'm capable of typing in a phone number.'

'Point taken,' Lucy said dryly. 'I wasn't saying that you were stupid—more that it's easy to accidentally type the wrong number. There must be another way of getting in touch with her.'

'How? I don't even know her last name. I know next to nothing about her; we didn't talk about personal stuff. The organisers of the event can't give me her name because of Data Protection rules.'

'True, but they could pass a message to her. Or you could put a message on social media.

It'd go viral because it's the sort of mystery people love solving. I can see it now.' She drew a banner in the air with her hands and intoned, 'Help Harry find his Lady in Red.'

Harry couldn't think of anything more horrific than having his love life plastered all over the media. He'd been there and done that during his divorce, and he had no intention of repeating the experience. 'No, thanks.'

'There might be a good reason why she couldn't meet you,' Lucy said. 'And you said her phone battery was flat, so she didn't have your number. That's why she couldn't ring you.'

'And that's where your theory falls down,' Harry said. 'She knew I was playing at the hall on the Saturday night. If she'd looked up the details of the ball, she could've sent me a message through our website. She hasn't—so she's not interested. She ghosted me. It's not very nice.' It had made him feel horrible. 'But I just have to accept it and move on.'

'Oh, Harry.' Lucy ruffled his hair. 'I know it went wrong with Rochelle, but history isn't going to repeat itself.'

Absolutely—because he wasn't going to let that happen. Ever.

'I'm not being stubborn,' he fibbed. 'It's fine. And please don't do anything to embarrass me on social media, Lucy. I mean it.' He didn't need a relationship. And he'd make the same choice that he made last time: his career, rather than his love life. He knew where he was with music.

'OK, Holls. You know the drill from last year,' Shauna, the nurse at the university clinic, said. 'I ask you if you're pregnant, you tell me that you're not, and then I give you the malaria tablets and off you go on your trip to Egypt.'

Holly smiled. 'OK. I'm n—' She stopped. When had her last period been? She thought back. Two months.

Two months.

'Can being knocked over by a car stop your periods?' she asked. 'Because of shock or something like that?'

'It's possible, but it's not the most likely cause of a missed period.'

No. They both knew what *that* was.

Shauna looked at her. 'How many have you missed?'

'Two.' Holly had been so busy at work, she hadn't really thought about anything else.

'Could you be pregnant?'

She shook her head. Simon had been in America for months before he'd called off their wedding. She hadn't dated anyone since they'd split up. She couldn't even remember the last time she'd actually had sex.

The best way to get over someone is to have a fling. Natalie's advice slid into her head. Along with her own text: I took your advice.

Had she? Had she *really* had a mad fling during her lost weekend, rather than just simply teasing her best friend about it?

She couldn't remember even meeting anyone, let alone having sex with him or using birth control…

'Holly?'

'I don't know,' she said. But it was beginning to look like a possibility.

'Have you had any other early pregnancy symptoms?' Shauna asked. 'Sore boobs, feeling really tired, needing to pee more, feeling sick?'

'I've felt a bit tired, but I'm pretty sure that's because of the accident,' Holly said.

'OK. Have you been sensitive to smells, had any cravings, or had any mood swings?'

Holly shook her head.

'Then go and buy a pregnancy test, just to be sure.' Shauna smiled at her. 'You're right, and it's probably the stress of the accident that's messed up your cycle, but I'm afraid we do need to make absolutely sure you're not pregnant before we can give you the malaria treatment. Which means you need to take a test—just to tick all the boxes.'

If the test said she was pregnant, that meant no malaria treatment. Which in turn meant no Egypt—and an awful lot to think about.

Holly took a deep breath. 'Go away and come back tomorrow, then?'

Shauna nodded. 'It's probably nothing to worry about. I'll book you in now.'

'OK. Thanks.' Holly walked out of the clinic and headed for the nearest supermarket to buy a pregnancy test.

She hadn't had even the slightest feeling of nausea. Her breasts felt completely normal. She'd put on a couple of pounds, but that was probably because she hadn't been to the gym since the accident. Her final check-up was next week and then life could go on as normal.

Pregnant?

Of course she wasn't.

But the idea niggled away at her. Supposing she *was* pregnant? Supposing she really *had* had a mad fling and they'd been so carried away that they hadn't thought about contraception, or maybe the condom had failed?

Then again, she had friends who'd been trying for months to get pregnant. One night, one baby? It wasn't that probable.

Though it *was* possible…

She took a deep breath, and headed for the toilets to skim-read the instructions.

She peed on the stick, then replaced the cap and stared at the screen. The hourglass symbol flashed to show that the test was working. Holly was sure it wasn't going to be positive, but somehow adrenaline seem to be coursing through her fingers, causing her hands to shake.

The hourglass stopped flashing.

Shockingly, the word 'Pregnant' was displayed on the screen. In bold. Very clear. But the hourglass was still flashing, so maybe it was waiting for the word 'not' to show up.

Holly squeezed her eyes tightly shut, just in case, then peered at the screen again. The word 'Pregnant' was still there, but this time there was some extra text. Not the 'not' she'd been hoping for, but '3+'—meaning that she was more than three weeks pregnant.

So she really *had* had a fling.

And now she was pregnant, with absolutely no idea who the father was and no way of getting in touch with him.

What on earth was she going to do?

She texted her best friend.

Need to meet you for lunch. Urgent.

To her relief, a text came back almost instantly, but dismay flooded through her when she read it.

Shooting today—no time for breaks—can meet you after?

Holly really wanted to talk about it now, but this evening would have to do.

Thanks. Meet you at your office. Let me know what time.

Just gone six?

Great. See you then.

Somehow Holly got through her lecture, and then a pastoral meeting with one of her students who was having a wobble and panicking about Finals. She spent the rest of the afternoon thinking about her situation and making lists of pros and cons; then, at six, she waited in the reception at Natalie's office.

Natalie came out, took one look at her and frowned. 'From the look on your face, gin is required—and lots of it.'

'No.' Gin wouldn't be good for the baby. 'Can we get something to eat?'

'Sure.' Natalie led her to a tucked-away pizzeria. Once they'd ordered, Natalie said, 'Out with it.'

There wasn't an easy way to say this, so Holly got straight to the point. 'It seems I wasn't teasing you and I *did* have a fling.'

Natalie blinked. 'He called you?'

'No.'

'Then how do you know?' She looked hopeful. 'You've got your memory back?'

'Unfortunately not.' Holly took a deep breath. 'I'm pregnant.'

Natalie was silent.

'Say something,' Holly begged.

'I don't know what to say. This was the last thing I expected you to tell me.' Natalie bit her lip. 'Are you all right?'

Holly nodded. 'No symptoms, apart from two missed periods—which I was too busy to notice. Shauna said I needed to do a pregnancy test before she could give me malaria tablets for the dig in Egypt. So I did.' She spread her hands. 'It was positive—which means no malaria tablets, and no Egypt.'

'What are you going to do?' Natalie asked.

'I don't know,' Holly said, trying to damp down the panic. 'I don't have a clue who the father is. I don't remember his name or even what he looked like.'

'Dark hair, blond, red? Blue eyes, grey, brown?'

'No idea,' Holly said.

'If your phone was out of charge,' Natalie said, 'maybe he wrote his number down for you?'

'I looked through my handbag. There was nothing with a phone number on it,' Holly said. It made her feel sick. 'He hasn't tried to ring me, so that proves he wasn't really interested.' She hadn't been enough to make her mystery man want more than a one-night stand.

She pushed her pizza away, no longer hungry. 'It's all I've really been able to think about this afternoon. So I made a list. My options are termination, adoption, or keeping the baby.'

'And have you decided what *you* want?' Natalie asked gently.

'I don't want a termination,' Holly said. 'I know it's mad, given I can't remember a thing about the baby's father. But it's not the baby's fault. And, if I'm honest, I was starting to get a bit broody when Simon left for New York.'

Natalie looked shocked. 'You never said.'

'I was hardly ready to admit it to myself, let alone to anyone else. Though I didn't get pregnant on purpose.' Holly sighed. 'I'd never judge a woman for having a termination, because I think you should do what's right for *you*. Nobody else has the right to tell you what to do with your own body. But a termination doesn't feel right for me. Neither does adoption.'

'So does that mean you're going to keep the baby?'

Holly bit her lip. 'I was supposed to get married to Simon and then have a baby with him. Except I wasn't enough for Simon.' Or her mystery man.

'Simon is an utter...' Natalie growled a pithy description. 'Of course you were enough. *He* was the one who wasn't good enough for *you*.'

'Thank you.' Though Holly didn't believe her. 'I know it's not going to be easy, being a single mum. But I'll have the support of my family and closest friends. I can juggle childcare with my job, provided I stick to digs within driving distance of home.'

'I want to be the baby's godmother,' Natalie said. 'And you can count on me for babysitting and holding your hand on wobbly days. No matter what.'

Holly scrubbed away the tears that suddenly threatened to fall. 'Thank you.'

'That's what best friends are for,' Natalie

said. 'But we need to try and find the baby's father.'

'How? That weekend's still almost a complete blank, and it's terrifying. I know some of what I did because there are photographs. But I don't remember doing any of it.'

'Maybe you could go and see a hypnotist to see if they can recover something?' Natalie suggested. 'Or ask the hall to put a message on their social media.'

'Saying what? "Gentlemen! Did you come to a ball here ten weeks ago and have sex with a woman in a red dress? Because she has some interesting news for you…"' Holly rolled her eyes.

'Well, maybe not quite that,' Natalie said with a grin. 'But how about, "Did you dance with a lady in red at the ball? She needs to get in touch." I bet it'd go viral.' She drew an invisible banner in the air. '"Help the Lady in Red find her mystery man."'

'I don't *want* it to go viral. I don't want to live my life in public,' Holly said. She wrinkled her nose. 'Let's say I gave him my number. It's two months and he hasn't got in touch. Which means he's not interested in me, so he's even less likely to be interested in the baby.'

'It's still worth a try,' Natalie said.

'I can manage on my own,' Holly insisted.

'You know, he must've been really amazing,' Natalie said. 'Because you're not the sort to have a fling for the sake of it.'

'If he was that amazing, surely I'd have remembered *something* about him by now?' Holly pointed out.

'You had a head injury,' Natalie reminded her. 'It might always be your lost weekend.' She paused. 'What about work?'

'The university will be fine about it,' Holly said. 'But I can't go to Egypt this summer. I also won't be able to do any work that involves radiology, because it isn't safe for the baby. I can do lectures, tutorials, and the desk side of things—and maybe the odd bit of work on a UK dig if I clear it with Health and Safety.' She rested her hand on her not-yet-showing bump. 'But hey. Nefertiti here—or Amenhotep—needs to come first.'

'You can't call that poor baby either of those names,' Natalie said, looking horrified.

'Nefertiti was allegedly the most beautiful woman in the world, even more so than Cleopatra, and Amenhotep III is my favourite pharaoh—the one who made his country prosperous and built amazing monuments,' Holly pointed out.

'I thought it was Khufu who built the pyramids?'

'He did,' Holly said with a smile. 'One of them, anyway.'

'All your colleagues are going to call the bump Mini-Lara or Mini-Indi,' Natalie said.

'And make jokes that instead of studying mummies, I'm going to *be* a mummy.' Holly swallowed hard. 'Which is weird. It's not quite how I thought things were going to turn out.'

'You don't have to make all your decisions now,' Natalie said.

'I kind of do. Two missed periods—that means I'm at least ten weeks gone. I need to see my GP, get booked in with the midwife, have a scan. And tell my family. And work. And…' Suddenly, the decision she'd come to that afternoon felt really, really daunting. Was she up to it? Would she even make a decent mum?

She must've spoken aloud, because Natalie said firmly, 'You're going to be brilliant. And you're not alone. You've got your family, you've got me, and you've got other friends who'll be there for you, too. Even though this baby wasn't planned, he or she is going to be really, really loved.' She grinned. 'And absolutely *not* called Nefertiti or Amenhotep…'

CHAPTER FOUR

'So you've got a team doing a dig at the abbey?' Harry asked at Monday lunchtime as his sister parked her car on the gravel in front of the house.

'When we started doing the footings for the Orangery extension, the team discovered bones. Luckily they turned out to be really old ones so it wasn't a crime scene, but obviously the area needs to be excavated and then we'll have the bones reburied in consecrated ground,' Ellen explained. 'The kids are all beyond excited and desperate to help— and the archaeologist in charge is absolutely lovely. She's great with kids. She's let them use brushes to help her team reveal little bits and pieces, and they've all decided they want to be archaeologists when they grow up, even though she's warned them that half the time it means being on your knees and covered in mud and finding nothing but a couple of rusty nails.

'George has been begging her to go to the British Museum with them to see the mummies, and Henry's borrowed a book on hieroglyphics and he's been writing notes to everyone in them. Even Alice and Celia want to dress up as Cleopatra all the time.'

'It sounds as if the kids all have Egypt mania.' Harry smiled. 'Dare I ask if our parents are behaving?'

'Once Pa finished harrumphing about the disruption,' Ellen said, 'Dr Weston got talking to him about the past and she's drawn him sketches of what the abbey might have looked like. And he's eating out of her hand. So is Ma. It's incredible.'

'The main thing is that they're not giving you and Dom any grief.'

'Apart from grumbling about how much money it's costing to extend the Orangery for the tea rooms and shop, no,' Ellen said. 'And Dom pointed out that we'll get extra visitors coming to see the dig. I think the figures have finally made Pa see sense. Any day now, he'll start claiming it was all his idea.'

'That's terrible, Nell.'

Ellen grinned. 'I don't mind. If it means he lets us just get on with things, then he can claim just about anything he pleases.' She tucked her hand into the crook of his arm.

actually tingled when he'd shaken her hand, she wasn't going to do anything about the attraction. He was way out of her league, and she wasn't in the market for a relationship anyway.

'I'm sorry I didn't recognise you,' Holly said politely. 'Nice to meet you, too.'

Why was he looking at her as if he'd seen a ghost? She was sure they'd never met before. Harry Moran was definitely not the sort of man you'd forget easily.

Sorry she didn't recognise him? Oh, for pity's sake. They'd spent the night together. Had breakfast together. Planned to have a touristy day together... Except then she hadn't turned up.

There wasn't the slightest hint of mockery in her eyes; but there was also no hint of acknowledging the night they'd spent together in Bath. Back then, he'd thought Holly was completely genuine, and his instincts were pretty good. So there had to be another explanation for why she was behaving as if she'd never seen him before in her life.

Did she have some kind of doppelgänger? A twin, perhaps? And, if so, was *this* Holly the good twin or the bad twin? Had he slept

'Come and meet the team. And I can get to show off my brilliant baby brother. Thinking about it, we can use this for you, too. We could shoot a promo video of you playing something haunting among the ruins...'

Harry chuckled. 'Are you planning to give up the biscuit business and become my manager?' he teased. 'Or are you planning it to be a biscuit promo?'

'Now there's an idea. We can rename Bach's cello suite as the Beckett's Custard Cream suite...'

They were still laughing when they rounded the corner and Harry saw the full extent of the trenches cutting across the area around the Orangery. The lawn was a wreck. There was mud everywhere. And then, emerging from a trench, there she was.

His mysterious Lady in Red.

Holly, the woman who had spent the night with him in Bath and then vanished.

It felt as if someone had just punched him in the stomach. Hard.

What on earth was she doing here?

All he could do was stare as his sister said cheerfully, 'Holly, this is my baby brother, Harry Moran. Harry, this is Dr Holly Weston, who's leading the team in the dig.'

There wasn't even a flicker of recognition

in Holly's face as she looked at him. 'Good afternoon, Mr Moran. Have you come to see the devastation we've wrought on your parents' garden?'

'I...' This was unbelievable. How could she just stand there and pretend they'd never met? He'd thought they'd had some kind of connection. For pity's sake, they'd spent the night together! Clearly he'd been wrong about there being anything between them. Lucy's theory about a good reason for his mysterious date not meeting him was completely wrong.

The truth was very obvious: Dr Holly Weston was a game-player, and their night together had meant absolutely nothing to her.

It left him reeling. He wasn't sure if he was more hurt or angry. But he sure as hell wasn't going to show it. If this was the way she wanted it, he would pretend she was a stranger, too. He forced himself to smile. 'Nice to meet you, Dr Weston,' he said coolly.

She wiped the dirt off her hand onto her T-shirt and held out her hand to shake his.

And Harry was horrified to realise that his palm was actually tingling when it touched hers. The attraction was still very much there on his part. He remembered how she'd felt in his arms, and the warmth of her mouth as it had touched his, and he really wanted to feel

that way again. But he'd just have to suppress the desire, because he didn't want to get involved with a game-player. No matter if her hair was like ripened corn and her eyes were an unusual amber colour. His heart had already been broken, and he wasn't letting that happen again.

Ellen's younger brother was nothing like her or their older brother, Dominic, Holly thought. There was no warmth in Harry Moran's smile, only a tightness. Great. Another member of the Moran family that she would have to charm. Clearly Harry took after his parents rather than his siblings when it came to being difficult.

'Harry's quite famous. He's a cellist,' Ellen said, sounding every inch the proud sister. 'And he's absolutely brilliant.'

So *that* was it. Harry Moran was put out because Holly hadn't recognised him. Poor little rich boy: tall, dark and handsome, with those stunning midnight-blue eyes, he was probably used to women falling at his feet, all starry-eyed and thrilled to bits to meet him.

Well, tough. She didn't fall at people's feet. Especially someone as difficult and self-important as Harry Moran seemed to be. Even though he was gorgeous and her skin had

with a woman who looked like Holly but had borrowed her name for some reason?

'I'd better get on,' she said brightly. 'Do let me know if you'd like me to talk you through any of the findings, Mr Moran.'

Harry opened his mouth to ask her if she had a twin, but nothing came out. Which was probably just as well, because a question like that was very, very incriminating, and it wasn't something he wanted to discuss in front of his older sister.

'It's really interesting, Harry,' Ellen said, clearly oblivious to the fact that Harry felt as if he'd just been flattened by a steamroller.

'Holly! Holly! I made you a picture.' George, Ellen's eldest child, ran over and handed her a picture of a mummy. 'It's like the one you would've dug up in Egypt.'

'That's brilliant, George.' Holly crouched down beside him, and went through all the things he'd included in the picture. 'You remembered everything we talked about yesterday. Well done.'

'Can I take it to show Henry?'

'Great idea. And Henry might be able to do some hieroglyphics with you to help you label things. Have a think about what you're going to name your mummy,' Holly said. 'Remember what we said about how their names were formed?'

'Yay!' George said, and rushed off.

His sister was absolutely right: Holly Weston was good with kids.

Not that that was an issue for him. He wasn't planning on having a long-term relationship and children after his disaster with Rochelle.

But his nephew had raised an intriguing question. 'Were you meant to be in Egypt?' he asked Holly.

'I was supposed to be on a team working in Egypt over the summer,' she explained. 'For various reasons, someone else in the department needed to swap with me. Though please don't think I'll do a poor job or regard this as a second-rate substitute, because what we're finding here is utterly thrilling.'

'That's good,' Harry said. 'I'd better let you get on. Sorry for holding you up.'

'Pleasure,' she said, and her smile sent an unexpected surge of desire through him.

So inappropriate.

He needed to get a grip.

After a duty visit to his parents—who for once weren't fighting or finding fault with their youngest child—and seeing his brother and sister-in-law, Harry headed back to Ellen's house. He adored his nephew and niece. Seeing them was always a tiny bit bitter-sweet, because if his own child had lived then he or she would've been smack in between six-year-old George and four-year-old Alice. Every so often Harry caught himself wondering what his son or daughter would have been like. What his marriage might have been like. He might even have settled here in the village, so his child would grow up with cousins, aunts and uncles as a large part of his or her life...

He shoved the thought away. Not now. Instead, he played a complicated game about pharaohs, mummies and camels that George and Alice had made up together, and after his sister and brother-in-law got back from work he spent the evening chatting with them.

But he lay awake for a long time that night, thinking about Holly Weston and wondering what to do about the situation. The sensible thing would be to ignore it, to behave as if they were complete strangers. But, at the same time, Holly drew him more than any woman he'd met before; despite his common sense warning him that he didn't do relationships, he couldn't quite let it go. Maybe if he could get to the bottom of why she was behaving as if Bath had never happened, he could work out what to do next.

What he needed was an excuse to talk to her.

'So are the archaeologists staying at the abbey?' he asked Ellen casually over breakfast.

'No, they're staying at the Beauchamp Arms.'

So he could casually drop into the village pub this evening for a drink... But that would only work if she was sitting in the bar. She'd suggested talking through their finds, so maybe that would be a better start. 'How long is it likely to be before you can carry on with your Orangery development?'

'The end of the summer,' Ellen said. 'Though that's fine. We're not ready to open yet, and the delay gives us time to finalise the route, the guidebook, the gift shop and the website. If necessary, we can use marquees and make the café a pop-up tea tent until we can extend the Orangery.' She paused. 'I know your quartet is booked up for at least two years in advance, but do you think you'd be able to slot us in for the opening here?'

'I'm sure we can shuffle things round, if the dates don't work for you. But you're wise to plan it now,' he said. 'Let me know and I'll give the others the heads-up so we can pencil it in.'

'Next April?' she suggested. 'I love the sound of the Regency ball you played at. Maybe we can talk Pa into doing something like that at the abbey.'

'We didn't play the actual ball,' he reminded her. 'We were outside on the bandstand in the middle of the lake—and there isn't a lake at the abbey, let alone a bandstand in the middle.' The event where he'd met Holly, and she'd turned his world upside down. 'If you're thinking of holding a dance in the house, that's fine. Just tell me what sort of thing you want and we'll come up with some ideas for a workable playlist. Or if you want music to fireworks outside, overlooking the garden, we know some really good pyrotechnics people who can set it up.'

'Wonderful.' She smiled at him. 'So how long are you planning to stay?'

As long as he could, because he needed to talk to Holly and work out what was going on. 'I'm playing on Friday and Saturday night, so I'll need to head back to London on Friday morning; but I'd love to stay until then, if that's OK with you?'

'Of course it is. It's not often we get to see you.'

'Thanks.' He smiled at her. 'Actually, as you're putting me up, why don't I babysit for you tomorrow night and send you and Tris out for a posh dinner? My treat.'

'That'd be really nice.' She hugged him. 'It's good to have you home.'

'It's good to be back,' he said, meaning it.

After Ellen and Tristan had left for work and to drop off their children at their friends' houses for a play date, Harry headed down to the Orangery, and discovered Holly on her own in a trench. Fate was definitely on his side this morning. 'Good morning,' he said brightly.

Holly looked up at him, and his pulse rate speeded up a notch. Her eyes were incredible. 'Good morning,' she replied.

'Can I get you a cup of coffee or anything?' he asked.

'No, I'm fine with water, but thank you for asking.'

She was being scrupulously polite with him, and he could guess why: he'd been so shocked to see her yesterday that he'd behaved like an idiot. If he explained why, it would be really awkward. He still hadn't quite worked out how to broach the subject of their night together, and he needed to be careful not to alienate her. One thing he was clear about, though: he needed to apologise. 'I'm sorry I was a bit unwelcoming yesterday,' he said.

Her expression gave nothing away. 'It's understandable. We're intruding and our work is making a bit of a mess of the grounds.'

'It's not that. I'm pretty sure I came across as a celebrity whose nose was out of joint at not being recognised,' he said. 'Which isn't who I am. What I do is all about the music, not about me. I'm incredibly lucky to be able to do what I love most in the world for a living, and it's not something I'd ever take for granted. So I apologise for being bratty.'

She inclined her head in recognition. 'Ellen said you play the cello.'

'I do, though my taste in music is a little broader than what we tend to play.'

She gestured to the radio playing at the edge of the trench. 'I work to old pop songs when I'm on a dig, though I do like some classical music.'

'We play old pop songs, too.' He took a chance. 'One of our popular ones is "Don't You Forget About Me".'

Not a flicker. He remembered playing that to her in Ferdy's flat.

Why wasn't she responding? There must be an obvious reason, but he couldn't work it out.

'Hey, Lara. I brought your banana,' one of her students said, coming up to join them.

'Lara?' Harry asked.

Holly rolled her eyes. 'My students think it's funny to call me Lara Croft.' She wagged her finger at the younger man. 'It's Dr Weston to you, Jamal.'

But the smile in her face and the gleam in her eye told Harry that she was teasing rather than being officious.

'Yeah, yeah—Lara,' Jamal said with a grin. He looked at Harry. 'Actually, Dr Weston's way better than Lara Croft. She's a real heroine.'

Holly squirmed. 'I'm perfectly ordinary.'

'You're a heroine,' Jamal repeated. 'Not many people would do what you did. He looked at Harry. 'A couple of months ago, she was in Bath.'

So this *was* his Holly, Harry thought, reeling.

'She rescued a little boy from the path of the car, but the car crashed into her, and she hit her head.'

'I'm absolutely fine,' Holly said, 'and I can assure you that I'll be absolutely meticulous about leading this dig.' She wrinkled her nose. 'The only real problem the accident caused was that I lost about a week's worth of memories.'

'You lost about a week's worth of memories,' Harry repeated, trying to take it in.

'Retrograde amnesia. It's when you lose memories from before your accident or traumatic event. It's the most recent memories that are generally a problem. I don't remember the accident, but from what I've been told I was lucky to get away with nothing more serious than a bit of bruising and memory loss,' Holly said.

The penny dropped.

If she'd been hit by the car when she'd been on the way to meet him, that explained why she hadn't turned up. It also explained why she hadn't got in touch with him that morning: she must've been in hospital, plus she hadn't had his phone number.

This was the missing piece of the puzzle. If Holly had lost a week's worth of memories before the accident, that would include the memory of meeting him. Which was a perfectly reasonable explanation for why she'd acted just now if she'd never met him before, and also for why she hadn't tried to find him via the hall and the string quartet's website. How could she try to find him if she couldn't remember him?

Relief flooded through him. So his instincts hadn't been wrong after all. Holly Weston *wasn't* a game-player; she simply had no memory of even meeting him, let alone spending the night with him.

'That's a pretty amazing thing to do, to rescue a child from the path of a car,' he said.

She shrugged it off. 'It's what anyone would've done. Anyway, I'm assuming you came here as there was something you wanted?'

'Yes—you offered to talk me through your findings yesterday, and I wondered when would be a good time for you?' he asked.

'I could do it now,' she began, but Jamal put a hand on her arm.

'Doc, I nearly forgot—Ricky needs you to come and check something.'

'OK. Later, then?' she said to Harry with a smile.

This was the perfect opportunity to get to know her again—and for her to get to know him. 'How about I bring us lunch?' he suggested.

'A sandwich would be nice. Thank you,' she said.

'See you here at one?'

'One,' she agreed. 'Sorry to be rude and rush off.'

He raised both hands. 'You're working and I'm interrupting. No apologies needed.'

He called into the deli and bakery at the

village for picnic supplies, then headed back to Ellen's and spent the rest of the morning on his laptop, researching retrograde amnesia.

Amnesia actually seemed to be quite common after a head injury. Either it was retrograde, when the person couldn't remember the past, or anterograde, when the person had trouble forming a new memory. And Harry found the whole subject of memory itself fascinating, particularly when he clicked on an article about music and memory. It told him which areas of the brain lit up while someone listened to music, and how they were the same areas that involved memory. Studies showed that playing music helped people to remember things, and could spark memories even in people who had a brain injury.

So could he perhaps jog Holly's memory with music?

The evidence said that people who used songs and music while studying found it easier to remember things, such as the 'ABC' song helping people work out the position of a letter in the alphabet. So maybe if he played something from the set he and the quartet had played at the lake, Holly might remember meeting him. If he played one of the pieces he'd played to her in Ferdy's apartment, would it give her a flashback to the night they'd spent together?

He could try.

The next thing he needed to work out was how he could play something for her. He could hardly just turn up next to her trench and start playing his cello as she worked. She'd think he was either a maniac or a stalker.

He'd start with getting to know her a little better—or, rather, letting her get to know him again. And then perhaps together they could find a way forward.

Holly spent the rest of the morning feeling weirdly fluttery. And it was all because of Harry Moran. There was definitely something about him, and it felt as if she already knew him—which was ridiculous. She'd never met him before. And the attraction was so inappropriate. Nobody here at the abbey apart from her own team knew about the baby; but she couldn't possibly start thinking this way about one man when she was pregnant by a man she couldn't even remember. This was much too complicated.

Her heart actually skipped a beat when he came to her trench at one o'clock precisely, carrying a proper wicker picnic basket and a tartan rug. If she'd offered to bring someone a sandwich for a lunch meeting, it would've been a prepacked sandwich from the nearest supermarket; but, then, Harry Moran was the son of a viscount, so of course he'd go beyond that.

'Hi,' he said, looking faintly flustered.

Did he feel this weird spark of attraction, too? Her heart skipped another beat before her common sense kicked in. She was a scruffy archaeologist. She hadn't been enough for Simon, and she certainly wouldn't be enough for a famous cellist from a very posh family. 'Hi,' she said, and her voice actually squeaked. How pathetic was that? She sneaked a glance; either he hadn't noticed or he was in a similar state to her, because he didn't look as if he was laughing at her. 'That looks very nice—and a bit impressive.'

He winced. 'Sorry. I didn't mean to go over the top. It's just how...'

How people in his world did things. 'It's lovely,' she said. 'Thank you.'

She helped him spread out the tartan rug, and when her hands accidentally touched his she felt a zing like an electric shock. Oh, help. Right now, she was way out of her depth.

The wicker hamper contained china, proper cutlery and two glasses, plus a sourdough loaf, Brie—her favourite, though right now she couldn't eat it—a bowl of tiny plum tomatoes still on the vine, sliced chicken and watercress.

'This looks fabulous. I feel very spoiled,' she said.

'Pleasure.' He looked pleased, she noticed. 'I wasn't sure whether you'd prefer wine or something soft, so I brought both.' He indicated the two bottles in the hamper.

'I'm working,' she said, glad of the excuse, 'so elderflower cordial is perfect.'

He clearly noticed that she didn't touch the Brie. 'Sorry. I should've thought to buy cheddar as well.'

Not wanting to explain that pregnant women shouldn't eat Brie, she said, 'Chicken, tomato and watercress is the best sandwich in the world. And this is one of the nicest picnics I've ever had.'

'I brought lemon drizzle cake as well,' he said.

'Oh, now you can *definitely* visit again,' she said with a grin. 'It's my favourite.'

This was so strange. Part of her was flustered by him, but part of her felt at ease with him, as if she'd known him for a while. 'Have we…?' she began, then stopped. There was no reason why their paths should have crossed before.

'Have we what?' he asked.

She shook her head. 'Ignore me. It just feels as if I know you. It's probably because I can see the resemblance between you, Dominic and Ellen.'

'Probably,' he agreed, though there was something in his expression she couldn't quite read.

'Well, I need to earn my lunch,' she said. 'I'm supposed to be telling you about the dig.'

'I know you've probably already explained this several times to different members of my family, but I'd love to know what you've uncovered about the abbey so far, he said. 'I always imagined the monks chanting plainsong, except none of us really know where the church once was.'

This was a safe subject. And if she concentrated on work she could push that swell of attraction to the back of her mind. 'Benedictine monasteries tend to be built to the same kind of layout. They had the church to the north, and they built the cloisters and the garth—that's the garden in the middle of the cloisters—on the south side of the church. The chapter house and dormitories would be on the east of the cloisters, the dining room and kitchen to the south, and the accommodation for visitors and the infirm to the west.' She grabbed her notepad and drew him a quick sketch.

'So where am I standing at the moment?'

'The west end of the church,' she said. 'Your house is roughly on the site of the chapter house, where they had meetings, and the living quarters of the monks.' She gestured to the building. 'I'm guessing there would be signs of the original building in the cellars, because the house obviously dates from after the Reformation. The cloisters run around the edge of the lawn, and the dining room and kitchen would be opposite us.' She gestured to the wall to their right. 'Your walled garden— a lot of the material was probably taken from the original west range.'

Holly Weston really knew what she was talking about. And her work was clearly her passion; she was lit up from the inside out as she talked to him, Harry thought.

Just like the gorgeous woman he'd met wearing a Regency dress.

And to think he'd asked her back then if she'd ever visited the Roman Baths. As an archaeologist, she'd probably done more than just visit the place; she'd probably studied the site. If she ever got her memory back, he rather hoped that little bit of embarrassment would stay quietly forgotten.

'That,' he said, 'is amazing.'

She looked pleased. 'You could've found any of that information on the Internet.'

'It's not the same as actually hearing it from someone who knows their subject. Someone who's passionate about their subject.'

She'd seemed almost on the cusp of getting her memory back when she'd started to ask if they knew each other. He should perhaps have told her then; but it hadn't felt like the right moment.

He couldn't think of a way to get back to the subject of her memory loss, when she said, 'It's a real thrill to be part of this. To put a story back together. To find things that haven't been seen for centuries.' She looked at him. 'Is it like that with what you do?'

He nodded. 'We're telling a story and painting pictures for the audience, pretty much interpreting what the composer felt when he or she wrote the music.' And this was perhaps his cue. 'Maybe I could play for you some time and show you what I mean.'

She looked wary. 'Maybe.'

Was she wary because she was single and thought he might be hitting on her, or because there was someone else in her life? But asking her directly felt too awkward. He needed to regroup. 'Cake,' he said, clearing away the remains of their picnic, 'and then I'd better get out of your hair. Though maybe I could drop in and be nosy again tomorrow?'

'I'd like that,' she said.

CHAPTER FIVE

THE NEXT DAY, Harry called in to the estate office to see his brother. 'I'm babysitting tonight for Nell and Tris,' he said, 'so how about tomorrow night I babysit for you and Sal and send you out to dinner? My treat. It means I get time to play with Henry and Celia, and I'll cook pizza for the three of us so you don't have to worry about feeding them before you go out.'

'That would be great,' Dominic said. 'How do I talk you into coming to stay more often?'

'I'll make more of an effort,' Harry said, meaning it. 'I'm just glad that you and Ellen both have your own houses rather than living in a wing at the abbey, so I don't have to stay *there*.'

'Actually, the parents have been a lot better since the dig started,' Dominic said.

'You mean they have to play nice in public,' Harry said with a wry smile, knowing that his parents were good at putting on a united front outside the family. 'So is it a huge disruption, having the dig here?'

'No. The archaeologists are a nice lot,' Dominic said. 'They work all hours, though.'

'They probably have to make the most of the good weather,' Harry suggested, remembering what Holly had said the previous day.

'They put up a tarpaulin when it rains,' Dominic said. 'Holly's lovely, but she's as much of a workaholic as you are.'

Something else they had in common. And then he had a brilliant idea: the perfect way to get to know her but make her feel safe with him. 'Dom, can I ask someone to have supper with me and the kids tomorrow?' he asked.

Dominic looked surprised. 'Sure. Do we get to meet her?'

'It's not *that* sort of supper.' Which was only half the truth. 'I want to know more about the dig, but it isn't fair to stop the team working so they can talk to me. I was thinking about asking Dr Weston to have supper with us and tell me all about the dig at the same time.'

'Good idea,' Dominic said.

'Thanks. I'll go and have a quick word with her now.' He smiled.

'And you'll show your face in the house?' Dominic asked pointedly.

'So Pa can tell me yet again that I'm a wastrel and I don't contribute to the estate in the slightest?' Harry rolled his eyes. 'Which means I'll end up playing angry music all afternoon to get it out of my system.'

'The one that sounds like a wasp?'

'Bumblebee,' Harry corrected with a grin, knowing that his brother meant the Rimsky-Korsakov piece. The one Rochelle had played a lot on the flute as her audition piece, though weirdly playing it on the cello didn't bring back memories of his ex-wife. The speed of the piece always helped him to work out a bad mood. 'Yeah, that would do it. Fast and cross. A minute and a half. And then some Radiohead.'

Dominic grinned back. 'You mean the stuff the rest of the quartet won't let you play in public but I really like?'

'Yup. Stella says I'm just showing off, playing the cello like a guitar, but I love the music.'

'I'm almost tempted to skive off today, just to listen. I don't get to hear you play anywhere near as often as I'd like,' Dominic said.

Harry clapped his shoulder. 'All right. I promise I'll see the parents before I go. And

I'll bring my cello with me tomorrow night and play whatever you want before you and Sal go out. Catch you later.'

He went out across the lawn to the dig site. Holly was working in a trench; as he drew nearer, he realised that she was humming along to something on the radio. Better still, it was a piece he knew—and it gave him the perfect opening to try jogging her memory. '*West Side Story* fan?' he asked.

She looked up and smiled. 'Absolutely. Apart from George Chakiris being impossibly gorgeous, how can anyone resist a song as lovely as "Somewhere"?'

'It's beautiful,' he said. 'So you're a fan of musicals?'

'Absolutely. I go to shows with my best friend as often as I can,' she said with a smile.

Just what he'd hoped she'd say. 'How about *Chitty Chitty Bang Bang*?'

Something flickered in the back of Holly's head. Not quite a memory or a feeling, but *something*. She couldn't quite put her finger on it. Maybe it was something she'd heard on the radio recently without really being aware of it. 'I think everyone knows the title song,' she said, and hummed it.

'"Hushabye Mountain" is my favourite

piece from the film,' Harry said. 'Arranged for the cello.'

She frowned. 'I don't remember that one.'

'Maybe I can play it for you sometime,' he said.

Was he flirting with her? Her breath caught. She was starting to like the man she was getting to know. More than like: he really drew her. In other circumstances, she would've been really tempted to flirt back. But she had the baby to think about; besides, she'd already made the mistake of punching above her weight before with Simon. Harry was even more good looking than her ex. What on earth would he see in someone as ordinary as her? If she hadn't been good enough for Simon, she certainly wouldn't be good enough for Harry Moran.

Maybe she should tell him that her partner was coming down to see her tomorrow, to make him back off to a safe distance. Then again, if one of her team overheard, they'd be daft enough to start grilling her about her fake boyfriend, and then that would expose the lie to Harry, making her feel even more stupid.

Before she could make up an excuse, he said, 'Actually, I'm babysitting Henry and Celia for Dom and Sal tomorrow evening, and I promised to play something for Dom before they go out so I'll have my cello with me. If you're not busy tomorrow night and you'd like to join the kids and me for pizza, I'll play something for you after they've gone to bed, and in return perhaps you'll let me grill you a bit more about the dig.'

Holly was silent for so long that he thought she was going to refuse.

And then she smiled. It lit up her whole face, to the point where he felt his pulse start to leap. Oh, help. This was dangerous. She wasn't like Rochelle; he knew that. But he'd lost faith in his own judgement where relationships were concerned. Maybe he was being an idiot, seeking Holly out like this. Or maybe this was his chance to see if she could help fill the gap in his life that he'd been ignoring but which was becoming more and more obvious. 'All right. I'd like that. I'll bring pudding. What do you suggest?'

'Strawberries,' he said promptly. 'Because there's nothing better.' Would she remember that he'd given her strawberries for breakfast?

Apparently not, because there wasn't the slightest flicker of recognition in her face. 'Strawberries are fine by me,' she said.

'Great. The kids eat early, so shall we say half-past five tomorrow?' he asked.

'That'd be great.' Funny how the light in her eyes made the world feel suddenly bright.

'Good. I'll see you tomorrow,' he said.

Harry thoroughly enjoyed babysitting George and Alice that evening. He read them stories, he listened to them play what they'd been learning at their piano lessons, he played bits for them on the cello, and he taught them to do a round, playing 'Three Blind Mice' with them on the piano and himself on the cello. All the kind of things he'd once thought to do with his own child, but which he could still enjoy them with his nieces and nephews.

When they were finally asleep, Harry curled up in a chair and listened to music, a mug of peppermint tea by his side. Funny how his sister's house felt so much more of a home than his London flat did. There were photographs everywhere, well-loved books on the shelves, and a huge toy chest.

Despite their own upbringing, his sister was a brilliant mother, always having time for her children. His brother was the same. Harry had hoped to be like them when he'd come to terms with Rochelle's shock news about her pregnancy. Of course he'd done the right thing and married her. Except it had been the wrong thing.

How much of the break-up had been his fault?

It wasn't anyone's fault that she'd lost the baby. But he hadn't been there enough for her. He'd focused on his career, even though he'd known that cellists had a lot more openings than flautists. He should've made more compromises, let someone else take over from him in the quartet, and maybe taught instead of touring. Especially after the miscarriage, when he should have been there. You could replace a colleague a lot more easily than you could replace a partner.

But then, after that last fight, when Rochelle had told him that she'd got pregnant on purpose, and when he'd thought about her trying to persuade him to do less with his music and more with his family... Then he'd realised that she'd never really seen him for himself or loved him for himself. She'd wanted to be part of the aristocratic circles his family moved in, and when her career had stalled she'd been resentful that his was taking off. She'd wanted him to give up his music and work with his brother on the family estate.

Which wasn't what Harry had wanted at

all. She'd given him an ultimatum: his music or her. And Harry, completely disillusioned, had walked away.

Since his divorce, Harry had thrown himself into his music—the real love of his life—and he'd been lucky enough to be in the right place at the right time and able to take those opportunities.

Yet sometimes when he woke in the middle of the night, he felt that there was something missing. He could see how much happiness his siblings had found with their partners and children. Given Rochelle's revelation, the chances were that even if they hadn't lost the baby their marriage wouldn't have lasted. But still he wondered. Would he ever find someone who he could make happy and would make him happy, too?

Given that he hadn't been able to make a marriage work with someone who'd known him since he was eighteen—even though he realised with hindsight she hadn't really loved him—it seemed crazy to think that he could base any kind of future on something that had been literally a one-night stand. If Holly hadn't been in that accident, and they'd met up as planned, they might have had a chance to see where their relationship could go; and that might well have been a dead-end. A musician's life could be too peripatetic for a relationship to work.

On the other hand, he hadn't been able to get Holly out of his head, and he'd never felt like that about anyone else he'd ever met. Not even his ex-wife.

And then there was Holly's amnesia.

She only knew part of the truth. How would she react when he told her that he was part of the memories she'd lost? Would she back away? Would she be prepared to take a risk with him, especially as he didn't have a great track record with relationships? Would she think he was being creepy, or would she understand why he had held back from telling her the truth before now?

The thoughts went round and round in his head, and he just couldn't find a solution.

Harry couldn't settle to much on Thursday. And then finally it was time for him to go to Dominic and Sally's to babysit his niece and nephew. He'd bought pizza and salad earlier, as well as flowers for his sister-in-law.

'You really didn't need to, but thanks—they're gorgeous,' Sally said, kissing his cheek. 'Now, you know our number if—'

'—anything goes wrong. Which it won't,' he said firmly. 'Henry, Celia and I have plans.

ond, please?' she asked, and fled to the back door for fresh air.

Harry appeared beside her a few moments later. 'Are you all right?' he asked, looking concerned.

There was nothing for it. She was going to have to admit it. 'Just a touch of morning sickness. I thought I'd got away with it, but mine decided to start at ten weeks.' And she was sure it was psychosomatic: it had started on the very day she'd done the pregnancy test. 'I thought morning sickness was meant to stop at twelve weeks, but mine hasn't. It's just certain smells.' She grimaced. 'Normally I love garlic bread, but right now it doesn't love me.'

'Let me get you some water,' Harry said.

'But the children—'

'—are fine,' he said. 'Hopefully they'll have scoffed the garlic bread by the time you feel ready to go back in, but if they haven't I'll get rid of it.'

His kindness made her want to cry. It also made her feel sad, because now he knew about the baby the flirting would stop; anything else would be too complicated.

Holly was pregnant?

Harry's mind was in a whirl as he filled

Which involves scoffing lots of pizza, playing lots of games, and a bit of music.'

'So Dom and I miss out on the music? That's so unfair.'

Harry smiled. 'That's why I came early. I promised Dom. I'll play something before you go. Your choice.'

'The bumblebee!' Henry shouted gleefully.

'You can choose something later,' Harry told his nephew. 'This one is all for your mum.'

'You know what I'm going to ask for,' Sally said.

Of course he did: the song he'd played in the church as she'd walked down the aisle to his brother. 'It's better as a duet so I have the lovely piano intro,' he pointed out.

'I don't care. I'll just pretend I can hear the piano,' she said with a grin.

He took his cello from its case, checked the tuning, and launched into Bryan Adams's 'Everything I Do (I Do it for You)'.

Dominic came downstairs and wrapped his arms around his wife. 'This brings back memories. The best day of my life.'

'My joint favourite gig,' Harry said. 'Playing at your wedding and Nell and Tris's—it doesn't get any better than that.'

'You've played at the Royal Albert Hall. Surely that has to be the best?' Sally asked.

'No. Family all the way,' Harry said. He was beginning to realise how important family was to him, his parents excepted. 'Now go and have fun. Your children and I have plans.'

'Play some more, Uncle Harry. *Please*,' Celia begged.

'I will. After supper,' he said. 'But first we have games…'

They were halfway through a very rowdy board game when Holly arrived.

'Can I get you a cup of tea or something cold?' Harry asked.

'I'm fine,' she said, and her smile was so sweet that his heart actually skipped a beat. 'I brought strawberries and some ice cream. I hope that's OK?'

'It's perfect. Thank you.'

'Holly! Come and play with us,' Henry said, taking Holly's hand.

Once the game was finished, Harry said, 'I'm going to put the pizza on. Supper's in ten minutes. Celia, Henry, can you put the game away, wash your hands and lay the table for me, please?'

'Yes, Uncle Harry,' they choroused.

Harry Moran was completely different from the man she'd thought he was when they'd first met, Holly thought. Tonight he was smil-

ing and relaxed, very much a hands-on uncle. And he was really good with the children.

It felt like being part of the family, with the children chattering and Harry encouraging them. For a second, Holly could almost imagine that this was how her future would be—a future she'd thought to have with Simon when she'd looked after her nephew and niece as a trial run for parenthood…

She pushed the thought away. Nothing could happen between her and Harry. She was pregnant with another man's baby; she didn't even know who the father was and she had no way of finding out. What man would want to take on that kind of complication?

Besides, he'd asked her here so she could tell him more about the dig.

He'd made it very clear that she was safe with him. This wasn't a date.

Though it was hard not to feel as if it was. His smile had made her heart feel as if it had done an anatomically impossible backflip.

Everything was fine until they sat down to eat. But Harry had made garlic bread, and the scent set off her nausea. She tried really hard to breathe shallowly so she couldn't smell the garlic, but it didn't work.

'I'm so sorry. Can you excuse me for a sec-

a glass with water. He'd thought he'd felt shocked enough by seeing her again, but finding out that she was pregnant… That was a huge thing. Really huge. So huge he couldn't think straight.

Just how pregnant was she? Her top was loose enough to hide any sign of a bump.

He counted backwards in his head. It was three months since they'd spent the night together, and Holly had just said she was still having morning sickness after twelve weeks.

So was the baby his?

The ground felt as if it had shifted under his feet—just as it had six years ago.

'Harry, I'm pregnant.' Rochelle's face, full of worry and panic.

The announcement had happened at the worst possible time for him, when the quartet had just been starting to take off and they'd had a massive tour booked. He couldn't possibly let his colleagues—his best friends—down by calling it all off.

Wanting to reassure Rochelle that he loved her and he'd do the right thing by her, he'd married her a month later. But he'd still gone on the tour, promising her that they'd have their honeymoon later. Looking back, he knew it really hadn't been the right way to start a marriage, but he'd been young and a bit clueless and so torn. If he'd let the quartet down, he would never have been able to forgive himself as they'd all worked so hard and they deserved their success.

If he'd stayed in London with Rochelle, and taught instead of playing, he knew he would probably have resented her for holding him back. He'd promised to come home at every opportunity; and he'd called Rochelle every single day. He'd sent her flowers and treats he'd thought she'd like. He'd tried to make *everything* work.

Then, two weeks after he'd left for the tour, the real nightmare had begun...

He shook himself. No. That had been then. This was now.

He knew he'd used contraception; he would never have been so reckless as to ignore that. This wasn't a repeat of the situation with Rochelle. He and Holly had never met before, and nobody would deliberately try to get pregnant by a complete stranger.

Another memory from that night flickered back. Holly been very careful to check that he was single, and he'd assumed that she was, too. Maybe his assumption had been wrong. Could she really have slept with him, knowing that she was already pregnant by another man?

Yet he was sure the woman he'd met in Bath wasn't like that. The woman he was getting to know all over again was lovely. Warm and sweet.

Then again, Rochelle had also been warm and sweet when they'd been students and after they'd started dating and moved in together. It had started out so well. But, oh, how quickly their love had turned sour.

Cross with himself, because she was his guest and he should be looking after her better instead of brooding, he handed her the glass of water, and waited for her to take a couple of sips. 'Better?' he asked.

She nodded. 'Thank you. I'm sorry.'

'Not a problem,' he said, wanting to reassure her. 'So you're through the first trimester?'

'Yes, I'm about fourteen weeks,' she said.

So the baby *had* to be his.

But knowing how complicated relationships could be, and wary from his experience with Rochelle, he couldn't help saying, 'Your partner must worry about you while you're working away.'

Her face shuttered. 'He isn't around.'

Meaning either the man had let her down—or he really was the father. It really wouldn't be tactful to probe any more right now. Besides, how exactly was he going to say to her, 'Hey, you don't remember me, but I'm very probably the father of your baby'? Especially when the children might come in and over-hear. He was going to have to take this care-fully. Tactfully. 'I'm sorry. I didn't mean to pry.'

'I know. I'm sorry. I didn't mean to snap.'

'Let me deal with the dining table, and then come back with us,' he said.

Thankfully the children *had* scoffed all the garlic bread, and he was able to call Holly back to the table to finish her pizza and salad.

'Now will you play for us, Uncle Harry?' Henry asked when supper was over. 'Please?'

'Do you mind?' Harry asked, looking at Holly.

'It would be lovely,' she said.

'Clear the table for me, please, guys. I'll sort out the dishwasher later,' Harry directed, and went to wash his hands.

Holly helped the children, and when they went back to the dining room Harry had moved a chair next to the piano.

'Yesterday, George and Alice showed me what they were learning at piano lessons first, and then we played a bit together,' he said. 'Shall we do that?'

The children agreed enthusiastically. Celia played 'Who Said Mice?' from *Cats*, and Harry played 'The March of the Lion' from *The Carnival of Animals*.

Both Holly and Harry clapped loudly.

'Uncle Harry plays the really famous one from *The Carnival of Animals*,' Henry said.

'Oh, please play that one! I love it,' Celia said imploringly.

Harry spread his hands. 'All right, guys. Here we go.'

Holly was totally transfixed when he played 'The Swan', and the piece actually moved her to tears.

'Don't cry, Holly!' Celia fetched her a box of tissues.

'Thank you.' She took the tissues gratefully. 'That was so beautiful. Sorry for being wet.'

'That piece makes a lot of people cry,' Harry said.

There was something intense and searching in the way he looked at her, but Holly couldn't work out what he was looking for. She also couldn't work out why she felt something so familiar about the situation. Nobody had ever played a cello for her in a family home, she was sure. What was she half remembering?

'Let's do something a bit more upbeat,' Harry said. 'Celia, this is what I want you to play for four bars, and repeat.' He showed her, then let her play the four bars until he was happy that she was comfortable with the piece. 'Brilliant. Henry, this is your bit.' He played the melody, and let Henry practise that. 'Right. Let's do it together. And what do we do if we mess up a note?'

'Smile and keep going,' the children chorused.

'Excellent.' He winked at them, counted them in, and together they played 'Heart and Soul'.

'That was wonderful,' Holly said.

Harry gave her a speculative look. 'Do you play the piano, by any chance?'

'No,' she said.

'Then we'll teach you,' he said. 'We're going to play a round. Something everyone knows. "Frère Jacques".'

'But—' she began.

'It's easy, Holly,' Celia said. 'And it's fun.'

'We'll have the three of you at the piano. Henry at the bottom, Celia at the top, and Holly in the middle. Or,' he said, 'if you'd rather sing than play, Holly?'

'No, I'll have a go at the piano,' she said,

very aware of the expectant looks of the children. 'And if I miss a note...'

'Smile and keep going,' the children chorused.

She sat in the middle of the piano stool and Harry showed her the note pattern, breaking it down into manageable chunks for her and correcting her gently so she played the notes with the right fingers. He was kind, she noticed, and gentle. Qualities she really valued. And it made her blink back unexpected tears.

'Are we ready for this? Celia first, then Holly, then Henry, then me,' Harry directed.

And then, before she knew it, the children were sitting either side of her and she was playing the round with Harry and the children.

'That was amazing,' she said when they'd finished. Totally absorbing. She could understand why Harry loved what he did.

'Do you want to hear how amazing?' Harry waved his phone at her.

'You recorded it?' she asked, shocked.

'Yup.' He smiled, and played the piece back.

To her surprise, all the notes were in the right places—including hers. 'Nobody in my family has ever played an instrument. This is...' She shook her head in disbelief.

Harry Moran was amazing. And he was brilliant with children. It made her wonder why he wasn't married with children of his own—though that was a question she couldn't ask. It was way too rude and intrusive. Not to mention being none of her business.

'More, please!' Henry begged.

Harry looked at his watch. 'One more. Then it's bedtime, or your mum and dad won't let me do this again.'

'Will you play "The Bumblebee"?' Henry asked.

'That's a bit excitable. I was looking for something calming.'

Henry looked devastated. 'But you said earlier you'd play it for me.'

'I know,' Celia said. '"The Bumblebee" is really short, so if you do that first you'll have time to do another little one. The one I really like. "Sis…"' Her face screwed up in concentration as she tried to remember the name of the piece, and then she shook her head and hummed it.

'"Sicilienne",' Harry said, getting her to repeat the word, then he effortlessly zoomed through 'The Flight of the Bumblebee' for Henry before slowing down for Fauré's 'Sicilienne'.

'Now, bed. Or else I will be toast!'

'With jam!' Henry said, and squealed with delight as Harry chased him out of the room.

Harry returned just long enough to apologise to Holly. 'Do you mind if I read them just one chapter of Harry Potter?'

'Actually, I'd be happy to read the story, if you like,' she said. 'I do that with my niece and nephew.'

'Thank you. Then I'll sort out the dishwasher while you do that,' he said.

She was halfway through reading the chapter when Harry came up to join her. When she'd finished the chapter and Harry had kissed the children goodnight, they headed downstairs.

'You were very good with them,' he said. 'I think you'll be an amazing mum.'

There was something wistful in his expression. So did he have kids he didn't see, or did he perhaps want kids but couldn't have them and so he'd thrown himself into his music?

'Thank you. I hope that getting in some practice as an aunt will help,' she said lightly.

'I'm sure it will.'

She almost told him about her lost weekend, but she didn't want to risk spoiling things. Right now she felt safe with Harry. Cosseted. Valued, too. The way he looked at her… He made her feel attractive, something she wasn't used to, and she liked that feeling. Even though she knew it was wrong and it was selfish, she wanted more.

'Let me make us some tea, and then you can tell me all about the dig,' he said.

He made the tea just how she liked it—clearly, as a musician who played pieces without a score in front of him, he must have a good memory—and they settled in the living room at opposite ends of the sofa. She took him through what they'd found so far, and what she expected to find, and how they organised the work and catalogued the finds. And he did actually seem interested, asking questions every so often.

It was really easy to relax with Harry. She didn't know him very well, but she really liked what she'd seen of him so far. Plus he was gorgeous, even in jeans and a casual T-shirt; when he was dressed formally for work, no doubt all the women in the audience sighed over him.

Dressed maybe in historical costume: white pantaloons, a white shirt and cravat, a cream silk waistcoat and a navy tailcoat...

Where on earth had that come from?

She shook herself. How ridiculous.

'So what made you become an archaeologist?' he asked.

'My parents took me to the British Museum to see the mummies. And then there was an exhibition about Roman treasure—it was seeing the mosaic floors that thrilled me most,' she said. 'There was one with a peacock, and I just couldn't believe that someone had spent ages putting all those tiny tiles together to make a picture. And how amazing it must've been to discover it, to be the first person who'd seen it for centuries. From then on, I knew what I wanted to do.' She paused. 'Was it like that for you with music?'

'Granny Beckett—my mother's mother—played the piano,' he said. 'As soon as I could sit up, I used to point to the piano. She would let me sit on her lap and press the keys, and I loved it.' He smiled. 'Most kids like to watch cartoons and what have you, but I liked listening to music more than anything else in the world. I didn't care whether it was a recording or live. Granny Beckett had lots of Jacqueline du Pré records and she put one on. I was tiny—I must've been about five—and I was just transfixed when I heard du Pré playing the cello. Granny Beckett had a friend who taught the cello, and she came round one afternoon with a child-sized one so I could try it out. And that was it. The second I moved the bow across the strings,

I'd found what I was born to do. I've never looked back.'

'Your grandmother sounds like a really special woman,' Holly said, seeing the way his face lit up as he talked about her.

'She was,' Harry agreed. 'If it wasn't for her, I would probably have ended up in the family business, hating every second of it. But she pointed out that Dom would always be the heir, Nell was the one with the head for business who'd do well in the biscuit business, and I had a gift so I should be allowed to bring people the joy of music.' He smiled. 'It's one of the reasons why I like playing joint pieces with the kids. I loved doing duets with Granny Beckett, and the kids like doing the same thing with me.'

'Do you think any of them will end up following in your footsteps?' she asked.

'Maybe Henry. He's got a real feel for the piano. And even though he's the oldest and he'll eventually take over from Dominic, I know Dom would let Henry follow his dreams without any fights.'

Which told her that there had been a few fights with Harry's parents over his choice of career. 'I'm glad your grandmother supported you,' she said. 'I loved what you played earlier.'

'Thank you. I'm so grateful that I've been able to do what I love most in the world for a living,' he said. 'And I was privileged to play both my sister and my sister-in-law down the aisle on their wedding days.'

'Would you play something for me, or will it wake Henry and Celia?' she asked.

'It's fine. What would you like?'

'You mentioned a piece of music to me the other day.'

'"Hushabye Mountain".' His midnight-blue eyes were almost black. 'OK.'

They went back into the dining room. He gestured to her to have a seat; then he moved a chair, sat down and checked the cello's tuning before he began to play.

The music was beautiful, and Holly closed her eyes, letting the sounds draw pictures in her head. It was slow and sweet and soothing; yet at the same time it made her tingle. As if it was a prelude to something. Weirdly she was filled with the sensation of déjà vu, though she didn't understand why. Where on earth could she have heard this before? And why was it making her feel breathless and tingly? Was it the music, or was it something else? 'That's incredibly beautiful,' she said.

'It's really popular on the quartet's set list,' he said. He looked slightly sad, and she had no idea why, though she didn't want to be rude and ask.

'So you play at lots of different places?' she asked instead.

'Weddings, stately homes—we sometimes work with a company that does fireworks—and corporate events. We'll play pretty much any event, and we have a decent repertoire,' he said. 'Though my colleagues are more on the traditional side, and they get a bit cross with me when I mess about with radical arrangements.'

'What do you mean, radical?'

'Playing the cello like a guitar instead of with a bow,' he said.

'I don't get it,' she said.

'Neither,' he said with a sigh, 'do they.'

'No, I mean I don't get why they don't like it. Alan Rickman does it in *Truly Madly Deeply*, and it's one of my favourite film clips ever.'

'I know the one.' He looked at her. 'Do you know the words to that song?'

'Not all of them,' she admitted.

'Give me a sec.' He took his phone from his pocket, looked something up, and handed it to her. 'Here are the lyrics. Let's do it.' Then he picked up the cello and started to pluck the introduction to the song. It was just like the film. And all of a sudden Holly felt weak at the knees. This gorgeous, gorgeous man wanted to play a duet with her, mimicking one of the most romantic films she'd ever seen.

Her voice was a bit shaky at first as she began to sing 'The Sun Ain't Gonna Shine Any More', but grew stronger as he joined in. Even though he was a professional musician, he wasn't judging her or pointing out where she sang flat. He was singing with her, seeming to enjoy it as much as she was. This was *fun*.

And then, subtly, it changed. Every time she glanced up from the lyrics she noticed he was looking at her. Looking at her mouth, then catching her gaze: and it made her feel hot all over. By the end of the song she was actually quivering with yearning. Her gaze met his, and for a moment she thought he was going to lean over and kiss her.

If he did, there was no way she could stop herself kissing him back, baby or no baby. She wanted him. Really, really wanted him.

She felt her lips parting, and her skin tingled all over with anticipation. Her lower lip felt super-sensitive.

Moth to a flame.

He reached out and rubbed the pad of his

thumb against her lower lip, and excitement coiled deep in her belly. Everything was forgotten except this moment, this feeling, this connection. She was dimly aware of Harry propping the cello against the piano, and then somehow he was sitting next to her on the piano stool, his arms were wrapped around her waist, her fingers were tangled in his hair and her wrists resting against the nape of his neck, and he was kissing her—*really* kissing her.

And it felt like fireworks going off overhead. Sparkles of silver and pink and gold.

When he broke the kiss, she was shaking. It felt really familiar—but how could it? She'd known him for a matter of days, not a lifetime. They'd never kissed before. This couldn't feel so right.

Oh, help. He'd really done it now. He'd rushed in and kissed her when he should've given her time. At the very least he should have told her about the night she'd forgotten. The night that the accident had wiped out of her memory.

Right now, she looked slightly dazed.

Did she remember what had happened in Bath? Had the kiss and the music he'd played her been enough to unlock her memories?

But she didn't say a word.

And Harry didn't know what to say.

'I'm sorry,' he said at last. 'I shouldn't have done that.'

She flushed. 'No.'

'I...' He blew out a breath. 'I don't usually behave like this. I know it's no excuse, but there's something about you that just draws me.'

She inclined her head. 'It wasn't just you. Look, let's just put it down to the music and the way it stirs up emotions.'

Tell her now.

Except he couldn't. Not when she was right in the middle of sticking up a huge wall between them. How did he tell her that he believed he was the father of her baby? She'd think he was crazy and he didn't want her to push away even more.

'I, um, I'd better go,' she said.

'Normally, I'd see you safely home. That was what I'd originally planned to do when Dom and Sal came home tonight.'

She shook her head. 'You can't leave the children. You're babysitting.'

'Exactly. So will you let me call you a taxi?' he asked.

'It's only a ten-minute walk to the Beauchamp Arms, and it's still light outside.'

'Even so.' The last time he'd let her go without seeing her safely back to where she was staying, she'd been hit by a car. 'I'd feel happier. Please let me call you a taxi. And, just so you know, there are no strings, apart from the ones on the piano or my cello.'

She looked at him, smiling at his terrible pun; thankfully, it seemed he hadn't scared her off completely. 'All right. Thank you.'

He made a swift call. 'It's going to be twenty minutes,' he said. 'Which is long enough for me to make you another cup of tea, and maybe play something else. So my hands will be occupied and you can feel totally safe with me, because I don't want you to feel worried or uncomfortable.'

'Thank you,' she said.

He made the quickest cup of tea in history. And then he had to hope that he could play the cello well enough to move her to the point of agreeing to see him again. 'What would you like me to play?' he asked.

'Anything,' she said.

Just what she'd said that first time. Right. He'd take a risk and try to jog her memory. 'This is a bit flashy,' he said, and proceeded to play Paganini's 'Caprice No. 24'.

'I know this from somewhere,' she said.

He held his breath. Would she make the connection?

But then she said, 'I must've heard it on the radio or something.'

'Probably,' he agreed, damping down the disappointment. Instead, he played Bach and Elgar until her taxi arrived, things he knew he hadn't played for her before.

'Thank you for a lovely evening,' she said.

He couldn't quite let it go, and took her hand. 'Holly, I'm going back to London to-morrow for the weekend. I'm playing tomor-row night in London and at a wedding on Saturday evening, but—your university's in London, Dom says, so I assume you live there?'

'I do,' she confirmed. 'I stay here during the week, but I go home at weekends.'

'Would you consider having lunch with me in London on Sunday?'

'I…' She curved her hand over her barely-there bump and wrinkled her nose.

'I know,' he said softly. 'But it's not an issue for me.' And maybe on Sunday he could tell her about Bath and that he was the father of her baby. 'Have lunch with me. Please.'

For a moment he thought she was going to refuse, but then she nodded. 'All right. Where and what time?'

'What time is good for you?' he asked.

'Half-past twelve?' she suggested.

'Half-past twelve,' he repeated. 'Where-abouts are you?'

'Camden,' she said.

'Would you prefer to eat somewhere in Camden? Or I could book a table somewhere and pick you up?'

'I'll meet you at the restaurant,' she said. 'Anywhere you like.'

He'd been here before, arranging a date with her; and he was beginning to think that Lucy's theory was right and he *had* mistyped her number in his phone. He wasn't going to make a mistake like that again. 'Text me your number, and I'll let you know where I've managed to book,' he said.

She pulled her phone out of her bag. 'Oh. It's out of charge.' She grimaced. 'Sorry. Everyone nags me about this. It's a habit I need to break.'

He handed his phone to her. 'If you put your number in there, I'll text you later.'

And, while she was doing that, he scribbled his own number down on the back of his business card. 'Just in case I manage to break my phone or something before I text you,' he said. 'If you haven't heard from me by tomorrow morning, it means I've done something stupid with my phone, not that I've changed my mind and I'm ghosting you.' The way he'd once thought she'd ghosted him.

'Got it,' she said. And how sweet her smile was. It made him ache.

The more time he spent with her, the more he realised that he could be himself, with her. He really, really liked her.

But so much could go wrong. He'd thought that he and Rochelle would make a go of it, having so much in common and having known each other for years, but he'd been very wrong. Holly was nothing like Rochelle—and nothing like his parents with their constant fights—but he found it hard to ignore the past and how miserable relationships had made him.

He pulled himself together. 'All right. I'll see you on Sunday.'

He wanted to kiss her again. Really, *really* wanted to kiss her. But he didn't want to scare her away, so he let her go and finished clearing up before his brother and sister-in-law came home. He needed to tell Holly the truth about her lost weekend. But how?

Holly was thoughtful all the way back to the Beauchamp Arms. All evening, on and off, she'd felt this strange sense of déjà vu. As if she was on the cusp of something.

It absolutely wouldn't be fair of her to start any kind of relationship with Harry Moran. She was pregnant and she couldn't expect him to step into the place of the baby's father. Especially as she didn't even know who the baby's father was, which made her feel ashamed and guilty—though the sensible side of her knew that her amnesia wasn't her fault. And yet there was something about him. Something that drew her. He was nice. Kind. A real family man, clearly very fond of his nieces and nephews. Which rather begged the question of why he was still single and childless.

At the pub, she discovered that Harry had already paid for her taxi. That was definitely above and beyond. She texted him swiftly.

Thank you—though I could've paid for my own taxi.

It was the least I could do, as I wasn't able to drive you home myself.

An old-fashioned gallant gentleman.
Gallant…gentleman. Why was that familiar? Where had she heard that recently?
But it was like reaching out to grab mist

on the surface of a pond, gone again before she could think about it.

She curled up in bed and looked him up on the Internet.

Harry Moran. Cellist. Part of the Quartus string quartet, though he'd also released solo music. The youngest son of Viscount Moran.

He kept his private life very private, she noticed. It seemed as if he'd been married briefly, a few years ago, but all the articles that talked about his marriage were from the kind of gossip magazines she disliked. She'd rather hear Harry's side of the story from Harry himself, if he wanted to tell her.

All his social media talked about music, not necessarily played by him. The posts that talked about his awards and accolades were all by other people, tagging him in; he clearly wasn't one to boast about his achievements.

After reading his entire website and all the non-gossipy articles she could find about him, she still knew no more about Harry himself. She didn't have a clue what drove him, other than a love of music.

He'd seemed to be of the opinion that her baby wasn't a barrier to a future relationship with her. Why? Was he perhaps unable to have children of his own, and her baby would give him a ready-made family? Was that why his marriage had broken up? Though those weren't the kind of questions you could ask straight out. She needed to get to know him better before she asked.

Was she making the right decision, agreeing to meet him for lunch on Sunday? OK, so he'd said no strings... But did he really mean that?

There was only one way to find out: and that was to meet him on Sunday.

CHAPTER SIX

'YOU'VE ACTUALLY FOUND your Lady in Red?'
Lucy's eyes widened. 'Oh, my God! So did
you find out why she didn't turn up?'

'She was in a car accident,' Harry said,
'which meant she lost all her memories from
the week before it happened. Including meeting me.'

'Unbelievable! How did you find her?'

'She's leading the dig at the abbey.'

'Oh.' Lucy bit her lip. 'Awkward. So have
you told her?'

Harry wrinkled his nose. 'Not yet.'

'Why not?'

'It's complicated,' Harry said and focused
on tuning his cello, even though it didn't actually need it.

'How is it complicated?'

He couldn't quite bring himself to explain
about Holly being pregnant. Particularly as
Lucy knew all about why he'd married Ro-

chelle, and how he'd felt when she'd lost the baby. He'd sobbed his heart out on Lucy's shoulder over both the miscarriage and the divorce, though he'd kept the bit that had really broken him to himself.

'How am I going to tell her, Luce? "Oh, by the way, you also met me a few months ago and we spent the night together."' He rolled his eyes. 'That's going to go down well. Not.'

'If you don't tell her, when she finds out some other way—say she gets her memory back—it's going to be a whole lot worse,' Lucy warned. 'And don't fall back on the excuse that you're rubbish at emotional stuff because you're male and you're posh.'

'It's not an excuse. It's a fact.' It was one of the accusations Rochelle had hurled at him: that he backed away and lost himself in music rather than confronting anything. He'd grown up with his parents sniping at each other constantly and he'd hated the atmosphere, so he didn't seek out confrontations. And maybe deep down he'd used the tour as an excuse to stay away and avoid his own pain instead of coming back to comfort her.

The irony was that he'd won critical acclaim for his recording of Elgar's cello concerto later that year. He'd poured all his pain and his loss and the longing and the misery into his performance, letting the music comfort him.

When she'd finally told him the truth, it had hurt him so deeply that he hadn't let anyone else close since. How could he trust their motives for wanting to be close to him? How could he trust his own judgement, when he'd been so completely fooled? He'd loved her and he'd thought she'd loved him: but it had turned out he hadn't really known her at all.

He pushed the thought away. 'And you were right. When I put Holly's number in my phone, I got it wrong.'

'Told you so.' Lucy clapped him on the shoulder. 'You need to be honest with her. Yes, it's going to be awkward. But if you don't tell her, Harry, it'll come back to bite you.'

'I know.' He plucked the strings of the cello, subconsciously playing the song he and Holly had sung to, right before he'd kissed her again. 'I didn't expect this to *matter*, Luce. I barely know her. And I don't believe in love at first sight.'

'You don't believe in love, full stop,' she said. 'But it's out there. Ignore your parents, because they're really not like normal people. Ignore Rochelle, too, because she was just as much to blame for your marriage breaking up as you were.'

He knew that—they'd both been young, both made made decisions—but he still felt responsible.

'I have a long memory, and a good one,' she said softly. 'Yes, you could've done things differently. But so could she.'

Yeah. And Lucy didn't even know the worst of it. He hadn't told anyone about Rochelle deliberately getting pregnant. He didn't want to risk his heart to the care of anyone else ever again. Yes, he'd dated since his divorce; but he'd been wary since Rochelle's revelations, and he'd quickly discovered that his dates had seen him primarily either as Viscount Moran's youngest son or as Harry the up-and-coming celebrity musician. He just hadn't felt enough for any of them to want to break through the barriers and see if love could ever be real.

'Look at your brother and your sister,' Lucy continued. 'That's real. Look at Stella and Drew—that's real. Look at me and Carina. That's real, and we make it work even though I tour a lot and she's here in London.'

But his relationship with Rochelle hadn't been real. It had turned out that she hadn't loved him the way he'd thought she had. She'd found herself struggling to get work and to move up the ladder, and she'd wanted financial security so, shortly after she'd persuaded him to let her move in with him, she'd deliberately got pregnant, knowing that Harry would insist on marrying her—and gambling that he'd give up touring and instead work on his family's estate.

He'd done half of it, giving her the financial security she'd wanted. But he hadn't given up his career. His music was who he was. And her ultimatum to him, making him choose between her and his music, had backfired on her spectacularly.

When he said nothing, Lucy continued, 'Love *is* out there, Harry. And your Lady in Red—'

'—Holly,' he supplied.

'Holly. Get to know her. Because she might just be The One.'

Even though he'd stopped believing in love, Holly Weston made him feel…

How did he feel? He wasn't sure, but it definitely wasn't like anything he'd felt before. It was unsettling and exhilarating at the same time. Was that love? Did she feel anything like that for him? Or, if she didn't feel that way now, could she learn to love him? Could this work out?

Dealing with emotional stuff always made him back away. It was terrifying. He gave

Lucy his best smile. 'I get why Carina loves you so much. I love you, too. But now's not the time to discuss this. We have work to do.'

'Agreed. Love you, too, Harry.' She ruffled his hair. 'Let's go play the wedding.'

He'd play his best. He'd always do his best for the client.

But tonight he'd lie awake and wonder what was going to be best for Holly, for their baby, and for himself.

On Sunday morning, Holly couldn't settle to anything.

Was this a date, or wasn't it?

On the one hand, the way she'd felt when Harry had kissed her had been amazing. More than amazing. She'd never expected to feel like that.

On the other hand, she was pregnant with another man's baby. A man she couldn't even remember.

Harry had made it clear that the pregnancy wasn't an issue for him; but how could she start dating him, in the circumstances? Maybe she should've taken Natalie's advice and done something on social media to find her mystery man, because he had a right to know about the baby's existence—even though he hadn't contacted her at all since that weekend and she expected nothing from him.

She was still full of nerves when she took the tube to Clapham and found the restaurant where Harry had asked her to meet him. To her delight, it overlooked Clapham Common; the ceiling inside the restaurant was a canopy of flowers and there were fairy lights everywhere. The floors were stripped and sanded, the tables likewise, and the chairs were mismatched but somehow harmonious. She'd never seen anywhere so romantic and pretty.

Harry was already there, sitting at one of the tables, and he lifted his hand in acknowledgement as she scanned the room. When she walked over to join him, he stood up: an old-fashioned courtesy she really liked.

'Thank you for coming,' he said.

'Thank you for inviting me. This is lovely.' She gestured to the room.

'The food is amazing, too. On Sundays, they give you a choice of brunch or roast dinner.'

'Brunch for me, please,' she said. But there were so many things on the menu that she liked, she couldn't decide what to have.

'We could get a selection between us and share?' he suggested.

And suddenly everything was easy. 'That would be lovely.'

Once they'd ordered, she smiled at him. 'How did your concerts go?'

'Fine, thanks. We all enjoy playing weddings, and last night's set was fun. They chose "Rule the World" as the first dance, and the rest was a mix of pop songs—everything from the Beach Boys and the Beatles to Abba and Taylor Swift.' He grinned. 'Lucy was happy because she got a chance to show off her favourite Donna Summer track.'

'Did you get to use your cello as a guitar?'

He laughed. 'Sadly not. But it was a good night. Very different from the baroque pieces we played at St Martin's Church on Friday night, but I enjoyed playing those, too. I suppose I just love playing and sharing the sheer joy of music.' He smiled at her. 'How's the dig coming along?'

'It's fine. We're finding really interesting bits from where the original church was, under what's now your Orangery. Complete floor tiles, a couple of rather battered church vessels, some coins—and my absolute favourite, a tiny brass.' She took her phone from her pocket. 'I took some photos of the finds because I thought you might like to see them.'

'Absolutely.' He looked at the photographs

with her and asked tons of perceptive, intelligent questions; and he paid attention to her answers rather than just giving her a polite smile to conceal his boredom, as Simon often had.

Funny how easy it was to talk to Harry. She felt comfortable with him yet, at the same time, there was an undercurrent of excitement she couldn't remember feeling with anyone else before.

But she really needed to be fair to him rather than string him along.

She waited until they'd both finished their food and had a top-up of tea before saying, 'Harry, I need to be honest with you. I like you—' she liked him a lot '—but right now I'm not looking to date anyone. Given my circumstances, it isn't fair to let you think otherwise.'

'Thank you for being honest with me.' He took a deep breath. 'Have any of your memories from the week before your accident come back yet?'

'No, and it's been months now so they may never come back,' she said.

'Then I need to be honest with you, too,' he said.

Honest? Why? She looked at him, not understanding. 'What do you mean?'

'Quartus—my quartet—played an event just outside Bath a few months ago.'

She frowned. Her accident had happened in Bath. Was he saying…? It felt as if someone had just tipped a bucket of cold water onto her from a great height. 'Hang on. Are you telling me you played at the ball I had a ticket to but can't remember attending?'

He nodded.

'So you saw me there?' And, if he'd seen her, there was a chance that he'd also seen her mystery man and could help her track him down. 'And you saw the guy I was with?'

'You were on your own.'

'Oh.' Another blind avenue. Her stomach swooped in disappointment.

He looked really awkward now. 'Holly, I'm trying to tell you that you met *me*.'

She frowned. At Beauchamp Abbey, he hadn't mentioned that they'd met before. 'Why didn't you say something when your sister introduced us?'

'Because when I saw you again at the dig, you acted as if you'd never met me before.'

Now it suddenly made sense. That must be why he'd looked so put out when he'd met her again at Beauchamp Abbey and she hadn't acknowledged him. He must've thought she was playing some sort of game.

But if she'd been on her own when he'd met her…did that mean that *he* was her mystery man?

Knowing that she might be making a huge fool of herself but needing to know the truth, she asked, 'Are you saying that you and I did more than just talk? That we spent the night together?' Which would mean that he was the father of her baby. But she stopped processing that when a really nasty thought shoved it to one side. 'Were you there at the accident?' Oh, no. Had he been the man who'd driven the car that had hit her?

'Yes, you spent the night with me and, no, I wasn't there when the car hit you,' he said. 'I think it must have happened when you were on the way to meeting me.'

That led to a whole new raft of questions. 'So why didn't you ring me when I didn't meet you?' Had he been sulking, thinking that she'd stood him up?

'I did ring you. Well, I *tried* to,' he amended, 'but it seems I'd taken your number down wrongly. I got a guy in Scotland instead.'

And that was it? He'd just given up? 'But you could've called the hotel, or tried to contact me through my work—there aren't exactly a lot of archaeologists in the world called Holly Weston.'

'But you wouldn't let me take you back to your hotel, so I didn't know where you were staying, and we didn't exchange surnames. I had no idea what you did for a living because we didn't talk about it. So I had no way of finding you—apart from putting something on social media that would've ended up embarrassing us both.'

Which was exactly why Holly had rejected Natalie's suggestion of using social media.

Shame seared through her, making her cheeks feel scorching hot. What the hell had she been thinking, going off with a stranger who surname she hadn't even known? Yes, she'd been hurt and angry at Simon's betrayal, but that didn't mean she could totally ignore common sense. Natalie hadn't really been serious in her suggestion that Holly should get over Simon by having a mad fling.

'So we spent the night together?' she asked again, just in case this was all some weird mistake.

'Yes.'

She felt sick. 'Didn't we use contraception?'

'No, we did,' he said. 'But no contraception is a hundred per cent reliable.'

'So you're the father of my baby.' It was a deduction rather than a question.

'Unless you'd slept with someone else that

week—' At her withering glare, he added hastily, 'Then, yes. The dates tie up.'

No wonder he'd been so adamant that the baby wasn't an issue. *Because it was his baby.*

And she'd been feeling guilty about her attraction to him and tying herself in knots over it, while all along he'd known the truth. She'd even told him that she'd lost her memory, but he still hadn't bothered to enlighten her.

He'd lied to her. By omission, but it was still a lie.

And, after Simon, she'd had *enough* of men lying to her.

'Why didn't you say anything when you first saw me at the abbey?' she demanded.

'Because you didn't appear to recognise me at all. I thought you were…well, a player,' he admitted.

A player? She wasn't like that at all, and although she could sort of see where he was coming from, she also didn't agree. 'But Jamal told you about my accident and I told you about my memory loss. You could've said something then.'

'In front of your team?' He raised his eyebrows. 'Hardly. It was something I thought you'd rather discuss in private.'

'But you *did* see me in private. When you asked me to dinner.' When he'd played her that beautiful music and he'd kissed her and her head had felt as if it were full of rainbows. 'Why didn't you tell me then?'

'Because it was awkward and I didn't know how to tell you. Plus I'd just found out you were pregnant by me. I was reeling.' He blew out a breath. 'I'm trying to tell you now.'

In a public place—which went completely against what he'd just said about thinking she'd rather discuss this in private.

It made her want to cry. Big, fat, ugly tears. Anger and misery and hopelessness, all rolled into one. She'd liked him so much. And he'd turned out to be another man like Simon. A man who'd lied and who'd let her down.

'I can't deal with this,' she said.

And, even though she knew she was behaving badly, she pushed her chair back and walked out of the restaurant, ignoring his soft, 'Holly, wait! Please.'

Right now, she needed fresh air. And she wanted to be on her own so she could start to process this.

Harry stared after Holly's retreating back, frozen by shock.

That really couldn't have gone any worse. What did he do now?

He didn't have time to sit and think about

it: he needed to go after her right now if he was to have any chance of salvaging this. He went over to the cash register, emptied his wallet and left more than enough notes to cover the bill, apologised, and dashed out after Holly.

She'd insisted on meeting him here rather than letting him pick her up, so he had no idea where she lived—other than it was somewhere in Camden—or which direction she would take on leaving the restaurant. He gazed around frantically, and saw her stepping into a black cab just down the street.

Where were all the taxis when you needed them? Why wasn't one coming along the street right now so he could flag it down, jump in and say, 'Follow that cab!'? Her taxi drove off, and there was no way he could follow her on foot.

Still, he had her mobile number. *If* her phone was charged. He called her and the connection went straight through to her voicemail. 'Holly, it's Harry. I'm sorry. Please call me. We need to talk about the baby,' he said.

He left his number at the end of the message, even though he knew she had it. Then he started to send her a text to back it up. Even though right now part of him was annoyed that she hadn't given him a chance to

explain and he thought she was being unreasonable, he had to take into account the
fact that she was pregnant and full of hormones, and up until now she'd been dealing
with this on her own. Plus she'd had the accident that had robbed her of her memory.
His news would've been a massive shock. He
needed to cut her some slack.

Holly, please call me. We need to talk about
the baby.

That sounded threatening, which wasn't
his intention.

And about how I can support you, he added,
hoping that she wouldn't take that the wrong
way. That was the problem with words on a
screen. It was all too easy to mistake the tone.
He would so much rather do this face to face,
but she hadn't left him any choice.

As soon as her phone shrilled, Holly knew
who was calling her without having to check
the screen. She ignored it and let the call go
to her voicemail. A few moments later, her
phone pinged to signal an incoming text.

Right now, she didn't want to talk to Harry
Moran or hear what he had to say. She wanted
to get her head around the situation first.

The one person she would have discussed the situation with was Natalie, but her best friend was away for the weekend. And, much as Holly loved her mum and her sister, this wasn't something she wanted to discuss with them. Part of her was ashamed of having a wild fling with a stranger, and she didn't want her mum and her sister to think less of her.

She asked the driver to drop her at the next tube station and headed for Regent's Park. A walk in a green space was what she needed to help her analyse this like the scientist she was, unpicking the layers and working things out for herself. She switched her phone off completely, not wanting anyone to disturb her, and wandered amongst the roses while she pondered the situation.

Harry Moran was the father of her baby.

So why did she still not remember a thing about that night? When he'd kissed her the other night, it had felt like fireworks going off in her head. Had it been the same that night in Bath? And, if so, *how* could she still have no memories of it?

And why hadn't he told her about this before? Why had he waited the best part of a week?

Pushing the hurt and anger aside, she tried

to think about it from his point of view and piece together what had happened in Bath.

They'd spent the night together. It was out of character for her to have that kind of wild fling, and she had a feeling that Harry wasn't the sort to sleep around either. She didn't remember their fling—but she'd felt a huge pull of attraction towards him when she'd met him again at Beauchamp, even when she hadn't known that he was the man she'd had a fling with. He'd clearly felt it, too, or he wouldn't have kissed her again.

Harry didn't know where she was staying, so that meant they must have gone to wherever he was staying after the ball, rather than to her hotel. She still had no idea where that was, but it must've been within walking distance of her hotel. And she'd agreed to meet him later that morning—except on the way she'd rescued the little boy and been hit by the car, none of which she remembered.

He hadn't known about the accident and had obviously waited for her at wherever they'd agreed to meet. When she hadn't turned up, he'd tried to call her—but he'd got someone else's number.

According to him, they hadn't even exchanged surnames. How could she have gone off with someone whose name she didn't even know? How could *he*?

Heat flared through her cheeks again. She never, ever got swept away like that. The one *grand passion* moment in her life, and she couldn't even remember it. How ironic was that? And yet she'd felt swept away again that night when they'd sung together and he'd played for her. She'd had butterflies in her stomach when she'd got ready to meet him for lunch today.

He'd known nothing at all about her. Not her surname, not where she lived, not what she did for a living. So, realistically, the only way he could have traced her was if he'd put a 'find the mystery girl' type post on social media. Why hadn't he done that? He had a reasonably high profile in the classical music world. People would have picked it up and tried to help.

Then again, looking at it from his point of view: he'd waited for her and she'd stood him up. When he'd called her, it was the wrong number. Logically, he must have believed she'd given him the wrong number on purpose so he couldn't get in touch with her, that she'd ghosted him.

And then, the next time he'd met her, she'd behaved as if she'd never met him before.

From her point of view, she *hadn't* met him before. But he wasn't privy to that information. If it had been the other way round, how would she have felt? She thought about it. She would have assumed he was a player and would've been furious with him. It kind of fitted with the way he'd reacted to her, all starchy and cold.

But there was an explanation. One that he'd learned pretty quickly. As soon as Jamal had told him about the accident and she'd filled in the gap, he must've realised that was why she hadn't turned up, and that she had no memory of him.

What would she have done, in his shoes?

How did you tell someone that they had forgotten you—and forgotten your wild fling, too?

For all Harry knew, Holly could have met someone else and fallen in love in the weeks between their fling and then meeting him again—just as he could have done. So his choices would've been to pretend their fling had never happened at all, or to choose his time carefully and talk to her about it in private.

Harry had clearly done the maths and worked out for himself that the date of her baby's conception tied in with the date of the fling she couldn't remember. Clearly that was why he'd asked her to Sunday lunch in a quiet restaurant, on neutral territory; it was the nearest he could get to talking in private without discussing it at either of their homes.

Had she just been massively unfair to him?

Very probably, she had to admit.

So what were they going to do about it?

As the father of their baby, Harry had had rights. Morally, if not legally, he could share in decisions about the baby's upbringing, and see the baby.

Would he want that?

Given how she'd seen Harry behave with his nieces and nephews, she was pretty sure he would want to be a hands-on father. But she also knew that his job involved a lot of travelling. The logistics would need to be worked out carefully.

And what about her?

Harry remembered her 'lost weekend'. He knew what had happened between them—and he'd kissed her again since then. Did that mean he wanted the relationship to continue? And was it because he wanted her, or did he feel obliged because of the baby?

She'd been in a relationship where her partner had settled for her and then discovered she really wasn't enough for him. She'd learned from the experience, and no way did she want to be in that situation again.

So where did that leave them?

She could hardly avoid Harry, given that the dig she was leading was at his parents' home. Anyone who had the grit and determination to make a successful career in the arts wouldn't let something like this just drop. If she refused to speak to him, he'd probably come and sit in her trench and refuse to move until she *did* talk to him. Meaning the whole mess would become very public and embarrass everyone.

With a sigh, she switched her phone back on. One missed call, one voicemail and one text—and they were all from Harry.

She listened to the voicemail first.

'Holly, I'm sorry. Please call me. We need to talk about the baby.'

Guilt flooded through her. She'd been the one to walk out and she'd left him to settle the bill, yet he was the one apologising.

She read his text.

Holly, please call me. We need to talk about the baby. And how I can support you.

It was all very calm, very polite, and very reasonable.

And it left her feeling very much in the wrong.

She bit her lip. Right now, she owed Harry Moran an apology. And he was right: they did need to talk about the baby.

She dialled his number.

'Holly?' He sounded wary when he answered.

'Sorry for walking out on you,' she said. 'You're right. We need to talk about the baby.'

'It's your decision,' he said. 'Tell me where and when.'

He was being so nice that it brought tears to her eyes. 'I don't know.' Which was stupid. For pity's sake, she had a PhD. She wasn't stupid. Why couldn't she answer a simple question about where and when to meet him?

'When are you going back to the abbey?' he asked.

'Tomorrow morning.'

'Are you free this afternoon?'

'Yes.' She swallowed hard.

'Where are you?'

'In Regent's Park, by the roses. Where are you?'

'Still in Clapham, walking on the Common.'

Walking and thinking, like she was? Even though they had very different backgrounds and very different jobs, they seemed to react the same way to things. Perhaps that was a good sign.

'I'll jump in a cab and come to you,' he suggested. 'Find somewhere to sit, and text me to let me know exactly where you are. I'll be there as soon as I can.'

'All right. I'll meet you by the waterfall in the Japanese Garden,' she said.

'I'm on my way,' he said, and hung up.

CHAPTER SEVEN

THIS MEETING WAS going to be more crucial than the most important audition he'd ever had in his life, Harry thought. And he really needed to get it right. Holly had agreed to meet him to talk about the baby; if he messed that up, he wouldn't get a second chance.

He still hadn't quite got his head round the fact that he was going to be a father. He'd been here before, and it had gone so badly wrong; it scared him that it could go wrong again. Then again, if it went right it would still be scary. He adored his nieces and nephews, playing with them, spending quality time with them and playing music with them; but he'd never had to deal with sickness or tantrums or being so bone-deep tired that he couldn't think straight, the way his brother and sister had. Babysitting a child for a few hours was a far cry from being completely responsible for a child.

If the baby made it through the pregnancy.

His and Rochelle's baby hadn't. OK, so it didn't mean that history would repeat itself, but this time round he was more aware of the risks.

And then there was Holly herself.

How did you make a success of a relationship with someone you barely knew? He liked the woman he'd got to know so far, and the physical attraction was most definitely still there. But they barely knew each other, and he wasn't great at relationships. He'd adored Granny and Grandpa Beckett—his father's parents had died when Harry was small, so he couldn't remember them—and he loved his siblings. But his relationship with his parents was strained to the point where he avoided them as much as possible. His marriage had been a disaster and he hadn't let anyone close to him since.

He had no idea how this thing between himself and Holly would work. But he did know that they needed to have a very honest and potentially very painful discussion.

He checked his phone to find out exactly where the Japanese Garden was in Regent's Park. After the taxi had dropped him at the entrance to the park, he headed through the Jubilee Gates and down a narrow path.

Just as she'd promised, Holly was waiting by the waterfall.

'Good choice,' he said, glad she'd found a quiet spot in the park. 'Thank you for agreeing to meet me. I'm sorry about earlier. I really don't want to fight.'

'I'm sorry, too,' she said. 'I shouldn't have walked out on you.'

Hormones, probably, though he wasn't quite stupid enough to say that out loud.

'And I owe you for lunch,' she continued.

He flapped his hand. 'No, you don't. My suggestion, my bill.' He took a deep breath. 'I've been thinking about things from your point of view and you're right. I should've told you as soon as I met you again.'

She gave him a wry smile. 'I've been thinking about it from your point of view, too. When I didn't turn up and the number you'd taken down turned out not to be mine, you must've thought I'd ghosted you.'

'I did.' He looked rueful. 'But now I know you couldn't remember a thing about me, so how could you possibly have got in contact with me?'

'I still don't remember anything from the few days before the accident,' she said. 'I think it's always going to be my lost weekend. And that's terrifying—reaching out for something and it's just not there.'

'It must be a horrible feeling. I read up about retrograde amnesia. That's why I tried playing you some of the music from that night, in case it made a connection for you and helped you to remember.' He wrinkled his nose. 'I'm sorry. Perhaps I should've come straight out with it.'

'What were you going to say? "Hello, you don't remember me, but I'm the father of your baby."? I would've run a mile,' she said. 'I'm sorry for throwing a hissy fit.'

'I think we're on the same side,' he said. And there was one mistake he'd learned from. 'The first thing I want you to know is that I'll support you.'

She gave him a level stare. 'You don't want me to do a DNA test to prove the baby's yours?'

'No need. The dates tie up,' he said. 'And you give the impression that you're not in the habit of sleeping around.'

Her smile was wry. 'That's correct. I'm much too beige for that.'

He frowned, not understanding. 'Beige?'

She gestured to her hair and her eyes. 'Beige. And most of the time I'm covered in mud, also beige.'

He smiled. '"Beige" isn't how I'd describe you. Besides, you were wearing a red dress when I first met you. A Regency dress.'

A dress she couldn't remember wearing, but she'd taken a mirror selfie for Natalie, so she knew that bit was true.

'I think,' Holly said, 'I'd like to start by filling in the gaps in my memory, if you wouldn't mind.'

'Do you trust me to tell you the truth?' he asked.

She nodded. 'What reason do you have to lie to me about what happened?'

'None whatsoever,' he confirmed. 'I have no idea what you did during the day before you arrived at the ball, but I noticed you sitting on the bank, watching us, wearing your red dress. I don't normally even see the audience when I play, because I'm always so focused on the music, but I kept seeing you. So, when the set ended and we were back on dry land, I came to talk to you. It was getting a bit chilly, so I lent you my jacket. And you said I was very gallant.'

His jacket. *Gallant.* Goosebumps prickled over her skin. 'Were you wearing Regency clothes, too?'

'You remember?' His voice held a note of hope.

'No.' Not quite. But she'd had that idea of him wearing a tailcoat and pantaloons. Was it the beginning of a memory resurfacing, or just coincidence?

'We went into the house, where we stopped at the buffet table and then we watched the Regency dancers.'

She smiled. 'I have two left feet, so I know we didn't join them.'

'Actually, we did,' he corrected. 'Not the Regency stuff—we went to the other ball-room, where they were playing slightly more modern dance music. We danced quite a lot. And then it all slowed down.'

Dancing with him. 'I don't remember,' she whispered. 'Did I tread on your toes?'

'No. You followed my lead. It felt like dancing on air. The perfect fit. I've done a lot of formal dancing, in my time, and that kind of chemistry's rare. And then...' He took a breath. 'I kissed you, and you kissed me back.'

His eyes had gone very, very dark. So did that mean he still felt that pull of attraction towards her? The same attraction that had sent fireworks flaring through her head the last time he'd kissed her?

'Then we decided to get out of there. I drove you back to Bath, and I asked you to come back for a drink to the place where I was staying.'

Which was where his story stopped making sense. 'I never go off with strangers.'

'A stranger and his cello,' he said. 'Though I know what you mean. I don't go off with strangers either, or ask them to go off with me. Just…' He shook his head as if trying to find an explanation. 'There was something about you. I can't explain it. This doesn't normally happen to me. But I didn't want to say goodnight.'

She knew she must have felt the same, because she'd felt drawn to him ever since she'd seen him again. Even the first day, when he'd been formal and stuffy and cold, she'd *noticed* him.

'One of my old school friends has a flat in the Circus. We went back there and I made you a cup of tea. Builders' tea, no sugar.'

The bit about tea sounded accurate. But where they'd gone… 'A flat in the Circus?' She shook her head. 'No way could I forget something like that. Nat—my best friend—is a huge Jane Austen fan. I would've told her all about it. Texted her. Taken a photo, at the very least.'

He coughed. 'Neither of us looked at our phones. When we did, the next morning, your battery was flat.'

'Uh-huh.' That sounded accurate, too. Everyone nagged her about keeping her phone charged.

'You asked me to play something for you.'

'"Hushabye Mountain".'

His eyes widened. 'You remember?'

'No. You played that for me at your brother's house, and you just told me you tried to jog my memory with music, so I assume that was one of the pieces you played for me in Bath.'

'But you didn't remember it,' he said.

'It's not your fault.' Her breath caught. 'And then I stayed the night.' She'd had the fling she couldn't remember. The thing that had changed her life. And, even though she knew intellectually how retrograde amnesia worked, emotionally she couldn't quite get it. How could she possibly have forgotten the kind of feeling that was strong enough to make her act so far out of character?

He nodded. 'I went out to buy croissants for breakfast. And strawberries. I asked if we could do something together. We planned to meet outside the Pump Room—but you wouldn't let me drop you at your hotel. You insisted on walking.'

That sounded like her, too. Her mother always grumbled that Holly was too independent.

'Because your phone was flat, you gave me your number. Except obviously I didn't take it down correctly,' he finished.

'And then, on the way to meet you, I rescued a little boy from the road and got hit by a car. None of which I remember.'

'Which must be really scary.'

He understood. He wasn't judging her; he was trying to put himself in her shoes. 'It is,' she admitted. 'It's like a black hole. One that I'm probably never going to be able to fill. The more time that passes, the less likely it is I'll remember.'

He took her hand and squeezed it briefly. 'That's hard. But it isn't your fault, Holly.'

'It doesn't matter whether it's my fault or not. It's still a blank. And I hate it.' She grimaced. He'd filled in some of the gaps, and right now she didn't know what to think or what to feel. Everything was mixed-up and crazy. She rested her hand on her bump to ground herself.

'It must've been a real shock when you realised you were pregnant,' he said. 'When did you find out?'

'Two months later. I was busy at work—it was exam season—so I'd barely even registered the missed periods. I was all ready to pick up my malaria tablets for the Egypt trip, but the practice nurse asked me if I was pregnant. It was a routine question. Even then, I thought it must be the accident messing up my cycle—plus I didn't remember you or anything else about that weekend.' She swallowed hard. 'She said I needed to take a test, just to rule it out. And I discovered that I'd forgotten even more than I'd thought I had.'

'So you were prepared to bring up the baby on your own?'

'I looked at all the options, and that was the one that worked for me. My family, friends and colleagues are all supportive.' She paused. 'Now we're both up to speed with the situation, I guess.'

He raked a hand through his hair, and the dishevelled look suited him. It made him look younger and more approachable. 'I want to support you and the baby. The tricky thing is my job, because I'm away quite a lot. But I think we can make it work if we both compromise a bit.'

Compromise? She was glad he'd said he'd

be there for the baby—but what about her? How did he feel about her? She narrowed her eyes at him. 'What sort of compromise did you have in mind?'

'I don't want to be a distant parent.' He blew out a breath. 'I really wasn't expecting to be a parent. Obviously you weren't either.'

'No. But I've had more time than you to get used to the idea.'

'I've had a couple of days to think about it. And here we are. Near strangers. Expecting a baby together in about five and a half months.' He looked at her. 'I intend to be a good father. But I should warn you that I don't usually do relationships.'

Which meant what, exactly?

He took a deep breath. 'I'm divorced.'

She winced. 'I know.'

His face shuttered. 'You've seen the media?'

'Obviously I looked you up on the Internet,' she said. 'I saw the headlines, yes, but I didn't go into those sites to read the details because it felt like prying. I thought if you wanted me to know, you'd tell me.'

'Give that today's all about honesty,' he said, 'then, yes, you need to know. I met Rochelle when I was eighteen, when we were studying at the Academy, though we didn't get together until after we graduated.' He sighed. 'She was a flautist. There are a lot more opportunities for cellists than there are for flautists. When you start out, you have to go wherever the work is. Although we were both based in London, if she had the chance of playing for a touring opera or ballet company, she had to go. She might've been playing in Glasgow while I had a contract down in, say, Truro.' He shrugged. 'If we'd both managed to play for the same orchestra, or seen each other for more than a snatched day here or there, maybe we could've made it work. But we didn't. I was offered a lot more work than she was, so even when we were in London she didn't see that much of me.'

'I'm sorry.'

'It was messy,' he admitted. 'And I didn't do enough to save my marriage. The quartet had started to take off, and we were getting regular bookings. I said I'd support Rochelle—I had family money—so she didn't have to worry about struggling to find work. I said that maybe she could teach or something, be based in London all the time so we weren't at opposite sides of the country and might see more of each other. And she accused me of putting my career before hers.' A muscle worked in his jaw. 'Up to a point, that's true.

I could've offered to stay in London and teach and let her be the one to go touring.'

'But playing's what makes you feel alive,' she said. 'I see your face when you play. It's your heart and soul coming out of your fingers into the music.'

'Thank you,' he said, 'for understanding that. Rochelle didn't, even though she was a musician as well. Or maybe it was because we ended up in competition, instead of supporting each other. Though it must've been hard for her. She was just as good a musician as I was, and it must've felt bad to be the one who was struggling.' He looked sad. 'So it didn't work out.'

Holly had a feeling that there was more to it than that. Those blue, blue eyes had darkened with pain, as if it hadn't been an amicable split. Had his ex maybe had an affair? Though it would be unkind to probe. 'I'm sorry.'

'She wanted me to give it up and work on my family's estate. Which meant I had a choice,' he said. 'My career or my marriage. I chose my career.'

Was that a warning? Or was it something he regretted?

He looked at her. 'The night we first met— the night you don't remember—you asked me if I was single. Which sounds to me as if maybe you've been let down by someone.'

'Dated someone who turned out to be married, you mean? Not quite.' She grimaced. 'I was supposed to get married a couple of weeks after Bath.'

He looked horrified. 'Are you telling me that you went off with me while you were engaged to—?' He stopped. 'No. Of course not. That's not who you are. I don't need you to confirm that. I apologise. I'm letting what happened with Rochelle get in the way, and that's not fair to you.'

That definitely sounded like an affair. She knew how it felt to be cheated on. And she appreciated that he didn't think she was the type to cheat. 'Thank you,' she said. 'No. I was single, but I had been in a relationship for eight years. Simon went on secondment to New York for six months; and while he was there he fell in love with someone else. He called off the wedding three weeks before I went to Bath. I was supposed to go to Rome for my hen weekend that weekend, but obviously I cancelled that, too.'

He took her hand. 'I'm sorry about your ex. That's a really horrible thing to happen.'

'I seemed to spend all my time either apologising to people or feeling like the world's biggest failure,' she admitted. 'I never want to go through that again.' She paused. 'Fenella—the woman Simon fell in love with—was pregnant. Which is why he called it off between us.'

Harry winced. 'That's rough.'

'It could've been worse. He could've left me at the altar,' she said, 'or told me after we'd got married. And then things would've been even more complicated.'

'I'm so sorry someone treated you like that.' Harry frowned. 'Are you telling me that, even though he was the one to end things, he made you unpick all the arrangements?'

'For someone who had to be so precise in his job, he was hopeless when it came to organising things at home. If I'd left it to him, it… Well, things would've been forgotten or not cancelled properly, and…' She grimaced. 'It was just easier to sort it out myself.'

'I'd call that adding insult to injury.'

'It is what it is.' She shrugged. 'But I think it's why I reacted so badly to you not telling me the truth. My tolerance for lies is pretty much at zero after Simon.' She looked at him. 'You didn't tell me an untruth, but it was a lie by omission.'

'Noted, and I apologise again. You deserve

better than that. And you deserved better than that from Simon as well.'

'My best friend said that, too. She wanted to do something nice for me, and she knew how much I'd been looking forward to Rome. The Roman Baths in Bath were her idea of the nearest substitute. And it was nice of her.'

He smiled wryly. 'And to think I asked you if you'd visited the Baths.'

She smiled back. 'Obviously I didn't tell you I'd worked on the site as a student, or you would have had an idea what I did for a living and been able to look me up on the Internet.'

'Indeed.' He paused. 'So where do we go from here?'

What did he want? she wondered. For that matter, what did *she* want?

'Whatever you decide, I'll support you and the baby. Though that doesn't mean you're tied to me,' he added hastily.

So did that mean he wanted to try and make some kind of future with her, or not? Right now they were supposed to be being honest with each other. So she'd get this out in the open. 'If I'd met you outside the Pump Room that morning—and I'm fairly sure I did intend to meet you, because otherwise I would've made an excuse and told you I had to get back to London,' she said, 'what do you think would've happened?'

'We would've had a nice day doing touristy things,' he said. 'And, if we'd had the chance to get to know each other a bit more, I might have suggested meeting up with you in London and seeing where things took us.'

'And now?'

'We've kind of skipped a step. We've made a baby without having a real relationship first.' He paused. 'Maybe we can rewind a little bit and get to know each other properly. Go on dates, as if the baby isn't part of the equation.'

It all sounded sensible.

But he hadn't said how he felt about her, or asked how she felt about him. She had the distinct feeling that Harry Moran kept his heart under armed guard. It was understandable, given that his marriage had ended badly, but it was frustrating. If he wasn't prepared to take a chance, open up to her as she'd try to open up to him, it wouldn't work between them.

'There's only one thing,' he said. 'Weekends are pretty busy for me at the moment. The quartet has a wedding booked for just about every Saturday between now and the end of the summer, and we have other commitments in between. I'm based in London, but we travel around a fair bit.' He paused. 'Which means Sunday lunchtimes are probably the best time for me to see you, and London's the easiest place to meet. Does that work for you?'

This felt more like a business arrangement than a relationship.

And even though Holly had told herself she didn't want any more relationships after Simon's betrayal, she realised that actually she did. And Harry's view on the whole thing felt lukewarm.

Did she really want to get involved with someone who was emotionally unavailable—to risk falling for someone who might not ever be able to feel the same way about her as she was starting to feel about him? She'd spent eight years in a relationship where she had been the one who'd loved the other the most, and she didn't want to repeat that.

The alternative was to cut him out of her life, which wasn't fair. This was his baby, too. And the baby deserved to know both parents.

At her continued silence, Harry said softly, 'I know that probably sounds like too little, too late. But I don't want to make any promises I can't keep.'

'It feels a bit clinical,' she admitted. 'OK, so I don't remember our fling, but...' But she wasn't the sort of person to have a fling. Harry wasn't either; so surely the fact that they'd both acted so out of character *meant* something? 'Plus we made a baby. Unintentionally.'

'I like you,' he said. 'At least I like the bit of you I've got to know so far.' There was a glint of amusement in his eyes as he said, 'Except possibly the hormonal version of you that stomps off in a huff.'

'That,' she said, 'isn't fair.' Then she thought about it. 'Or maybe it is. I don't usually stomp off in a huff.'

'Your colleagues call you Lara Croft— which I'm guessing is because you're not scared of anything and you just roll your sleeves up and sort things out, quietly and methodically. I like that.'

'And you make people *feel* things,' she said. 'I like hearing you play.'

'That's a good place to start from,' he said. 'I can't promise you this is going to work out between us, because I don't have a good track record.'

Was he trying to tell her that there was more than one divorce in his past?

The question must've shown on her face, because he said, 'I've only been married once, and there haven't been a string of long-term girlfriends. Or even much of a string of short-term ones. It took me a while to put myself back together after the divorce, and my work schedule means I'm not very available.'

'Uh-huh.' She didn't know what to say. He was sounding more and more emotionally distant.

'But I'll try my hardest. And, whatever happens between you and me, I want to be a decent dad to our child.'

So her *grand passion* had fizzled out. Disappointment flooded through her. He didn't want a relationship and he was clearly going to see her as an obligation. That wasn't what she wanted. At all.

It must have shown on her face, because he said, 'Holly, you need to know I'm not good at emotional stuff. I grew up with my parents fighting constantly and I used to escape into my music—which is an explanation, not an excuse, because I'll take the blame where it's due and I made a mess of my marriage. I know you've been hurt and your ex lied to you, and I don't want to make a promise to you that I'm scared I won't be able to keep.'

'So are you saying you want to be with me, or not?' she asked.

'I'm saying I'd like to try. Neither of us usually does mad things, but we still had that fling. My head's all over the place right now, but I want to get to know you better. Not just on Sundays,' he said. 'It's not that far a drive from London to Beauchamp. I could maybe come and see you during the week. I could take you out for dinner or into Cambridge and we could go punting on the river.'

So he *did* want to try. He was just scared that it would all go wrong. She could understand that, and it made her feel a bit less awkward. And, because he was offering something, she felt it was her turn to offer something, too. 'Because I was a bit late finding out about the baby, I'm late for everything else, too. I've got a dating scan in London on Wednesday, if you're free.'

'I'll make sure I'm free,' he said. 'Thank you.' He paused. 'Would you mind if we kept this to ourselves for now?'

'To ourselves,' she repeated. Was this his way of telling her that he didn't think she was good enough for his family and he'd have to talk them round?

'Dominic and Ellen will be thrilled,' he said, as if guessing what she was worrying about. 'My parents see the world in a very different way from most, and I don't want them upsetting you.'

'Oh.' So it kind of was that he didn't think she was good enough.

'Right now,' he said softly, 'I need to get my head around the idea of being a parent. And it's easier to do that at a distance from my own parents. You've met them, so you know they can be difficult. Even though Nell says they're both eating out of your hand.'

'I think they accept me now,' she said. 'At least, as the head of the dig.'

'For what it's worth,' he said, 'Dom and Nell like you. A lot. And Granny Beckett would definitely have approved of you.'

'I see.'

He reached over and took her hand. 'Let's just give ourselves some time to get to know each other without any outside pressure.'

Even though she still felt insecure, there was the baby to consider. And they had to start somewhere.

'Perhaps,' he said, 'I could offer you tea and cake at my place.'

He was inviting her into his private space. Given that he'd told her he wasn't good at emotional stuff, it couldn't be easy for him to ask her there; he was making the effort and she appreciated that. 'That,' she said, 'would be nice.'

Harry's flat was the top floor of a Victorian three-storey house, and it was much smaller than Holly had expected. Everything was neat and tidy, but it felt more like a hotel apartment than a real home. The only personal things in evidence were the framed photographs on the mantelpiece and the top of his piano: wedding pictures of his siblings, pictures of his nieces and nephews, and a photograph of what was clearly the quartet at an award ceremony.

He made her a mug of tea just how she liked it, and sat next to her on the sofa.

'So you're a minimalist, then,' she said.

'I'm away a lot. It makes sense to keep everything very tidy,' he said. 'I'm assuming that means you're not?'

'Let's just say I have a few overflowing bookcases, lots of maps, and a collection of fossils on display, not to mention the fact that I often work on my knees in mud,' she said. 'And I was expecting you to have a lot of music.'

'It's mainly in digital format,' he explained, 'though I do have a cupboard full of Granny Beckett's vinyl.'

That was what worried her. Everything was a little bit *too* neat and tidy. How would he cope with it being disordered? 'Babies make a lot of chaos,' she said.

He grinned. 'Having two nephews and two nieces, I already have a rough idea about that.'

'And you don't mind?'

'No.' He looked at her. 'So tell me about you.'

'There isn't that much to tell. I'm the younger of two girls. Our parents are both on the cusp of retiring and planning to travel a lot; my sister has a son and a daughter. I don't have any pets, because if I'm on a dig that would mean putting a dog in kennels or getting my mum or sister to dog-sit, which doesn't seem fair.' She spread her hands. 'That's about it.'

'Maybe we ought to find a list of speed dating questions,' he suggested. 'It'll be a quick way of getting to know each other.' When she nodded, he did a quick search on his phone. 'Right. What makes you happy?'

'Work,' she said promptly. 'And my family and friends.'

'Snap,' he said. 'Next: do you prefer the city or the country?'

'Both,' she said. 'I love living in London—but I also enjoy it when a dig is in the middle of nowhere and all I can hear is birdsong. You?'

'Both,' he said. 'I love living in London, too, but I like punting down to Grantchester and wandering through the meadows.'

'Sounds nice,' she said.

'I'll take you there,' he promised, and consulted the list again. 'What are you reading at the moment?'

She winced. 'Something really nerdy. A book about facial reconstruction.'

'I think I've seen an article about that in one of the Sunday supplements. Isn't that where you find a skeleton and the artist can work out what the person actually looked like when they were alive?' he asked.

'Yes. It's fascinating. They make a 3D model of the skull, import it to a virtual sculpture system, and the artist then reconstructs the facial muscles. There's an amazing one at the Johns Hopkins in America—the Cohen Mummy. For decades, everyone thought it was a boy, but it turned out to be a woman.' She grabbed her own phone and found the pictures for him. 'And they managed to do that from a partial skull—the jawbone was missing.'

'That's absolutely amazing.' He looked at her. 'I can see why you love your subject.'

Simon had always zoned out a bit when she'd talked about work. Having a partner who was actually interested in what she did felt strange—though in a good way. 'What are you reading?' she asked.

'A biography of Bach,' he said. 'Though I

also like crime novels. Not the gore-fests—I like the ones where you get inside the characters' heads.'

'Me, too,' she said. 'There's a brilliant series about a forensic archaeologist. I'll lend it to you, if you haven't already read it.'

He smiled at her. 'Thanks.'

'What about TV?' she asked.

'I don't bother very much. I'd rather be at a concert,' he said. 'How about you?'

'Costume drama,' she said. 'My best friend absolutely loves Jane Austen, so I've seen every adaptation going.'

He looked at his phone. 'Lark or owl?'

'Lark,' she said.

He wrinkled his nose. 'I'm an owl. I think we're both going to have to compromise a bit there.' He checked the screen again. 'What makes you laugh?'

'Bad puns.' She looked at him. 'What's an archaeologist's favourite sort of joke?' At his shrug, she said, 'Pre-hysterical.'

He laughed. 'Love it. What's the difference between a fish and a piano?' When she shook her head, he said, 'You can't tuna fish…'

'I think,' she said, 'our nieces and nephews are all about to double their joke stock.'

'Sounds good to me,' he said. 'What's your ideal holiday?'

'Somewhere with lots of ruins and museums to explore,' she said promptly. 'Yours?'

'Somewhere with lots of concerts.'

'So not a beach holiday?'

He shuddered. 'That's my idea of a nightmare.'

'Mine, too.' She looked at him. 'So we have a lot of things in common.'

'Which is a really good start.'

True, but she wanted more. She wanted him to want her, not to feel obliged because of the baby.

'What time is the scan on Wednesday?' he asked.

'Half-past nine. I'll text you the details,' she said.

'Thank you. And are you going straight back to Beauchamp afterwards?'

'Possibly.'

'Or maybe you could come to a lunchtime concert with me first? Some of my friends are playing Mozart at St Martin's on Wednesday. We could grab something to eat in the crypt beforehand.'

He was asking her on a real date? Something that was both reassuring and exciting. Maybe he wasn't going to see her as an obligation after all. 'I'd like that,' she said. 'And maybe we can take your nephew and nieces to see the mummies at the British Museum at the weekend, if you're around on Sunday.'

'I'd like that,' he said. His eyes crinkled at the corners. 'We could make a list of all the things that you would like to do, and work our way through it.'

A list. He was really beginning to sound like a man after her own heart, which gave her hope. 'You're a planner?' she checked.

'Lists are my guilty pleasure,' he admitted.

'Mine, too.'

He persuaded her to stay a bit longer by playing the piano for her, some of the pieces that he'd already played her on the cello, and then he drove her back to her flat.

'I'll see you on Wednesday,' he said on her doorstep. 'Maybe I can pick you up from here and we can go in to the hospital together.'

Like a real couple.

Funny how that made her feel so warm inside.

'Goodnight, Holly.' He looked at her and his eyes darkened.

Was he going to kiss her?

For a moment, she thought he was going to take a step backwards. And then he cupped her face in his hands, his touch gentle. Her skin tingled where it made contact with his, and as he stared at her mouth she felt her lips parting.

Slowly, slowly, he dipped his head and his mouth brushed against hers. And it felt as if the dull evening suddenly turned Technicolor, with the brightness and the saturation both turned up to the max.

By the time he broke the kiss, she was shaking—and she could see a slash of colour across his cheekbones. He might not be saying it, but she knew that he was affected by this thing between them just as much as she was.

'See you on Wednesday,' he said, and stole another kiss—as if he was finding it as hard to tear himself away from her as she was finding it to let him go.

CHAPTER EIGHT

AND JUST LIKE that Holly found herself in a relationship again. Except this wasn't safe and familiar, like it had been with Simon. Even seeing Harry's name on her phone screen made her heart beat faster.

She imagined this was what dating was supposed to be like in your teens—not that she'd dated much back then. The headiness, the excitement. Not being able to stop thinking about him and how it felt when he kissed her. Was it the same for him? She was beginning to think that it might be, because on Monday Harry texted her a photograph of the church where he and the quartet were playing Haydn. On Tuesday he called her, just to say hello. And on Wednesday her doorbell rang at a quarter to eight in the morning, when they'd arranged to meet at half past to go to the hospital.

'Good morning.' Harry handed her a beautiful bouquet of roses. 'I know you're not going to be here to enjoy them again until Saturday, but I couldn't let today go without bringing you flowers.' He kissed her lightly. 'And I brought us breakfast.'

Which turned out to be freshly squeezed orange juice and still-warm croissants. 'Thank you. That's so lovel—' To her horror, Holly felt a tear slide down her cheek. She brushed it away with the back of her hand. 'Sorry. Hormones. I'm really not one of these women who cries buckets at every little thing.' But she wasn't used to feeling as if someone cherished her, and it threw her.

'I know you're not a weeper.' He kissed her again, his mouth warm and sweet and reassuring, yet at the same time it sent her pulse rate soaring. 'So are you OK?'

She nodded. 'I've just put the kettle on. I'm supposed to drink loads of water—'

'—before the scan,' he finished. 'I've been reading up on things.'

He ended up making the tea while she put the flowers in water.

When had someone last brought her flowers?

Apart from the ones all her visitors had brought her after the accident, she thought it was probably her mum on her birthday.

Simon hadn't been one for romantic gestures. And Holly was discovering that she liked romantic gestures. She liked them very much indeed.

Harry held her hand all the way to the tube station, all the way on the tube journey, and all the way to the hospital. And he kept his fingers laced tightly through her own in the waiting room, after he'd checked that she was comfortable and had water. Was he maybe nervous of hospitals? she wondered.

Harry felt sick. Adrenaline was speeding through his bloodstream. It was way, way worse than the nerves he always felt just as he walked onto the stage. But on a stage he knew what he was doing, plus he had his cello to cling to. Here, he had no control over whether things would go well or not. He was holding Holly's hand, and he knew he was holding it way too tightly, but he couldn't help himself.

The last time he'd been a prospective father, it had all gone so badly wrong. He hadn't even got to the stage of having the first scan with Rochelle, because she'd lost the baby two days before their appointment. Even if today turned out to be fine, so many things could still go wrong. Maybe it had been a mistake to search the Internet to find out what to expect at each stage of the pregnancy. Holly was past twelve weeks, so in theory she was out of the major danger zone, and the dating scan would give them an accurate figure. But supposing the sonographer couldn't find a heartbeat? Supposing, instead of happy tears, there was just despair, like last time?

He was older now. Wiser. He would handle things very differently if this turned out to be a crisis.

But until he heard the magic words, he wasn't taking anything for granted.

'Are you all right, Harry?' Holly asked.

'I'm fine,' he lied.

'Just… I can't feel my fingers.'

'Sorry.' He swallowed hard and forced himself to loosen his grip. 'I'm just a bit nervous. Which is ridiculous, I know, because you're the one actually carrying the baby and you're—'

'Harry,' she said softly, 'shut up.'

And then she kissed him.

It wasn't a passionate, earthy, no-holds-barred kiss. It was sweet and gentle and reassuring. Letting him know that, whatever happened, it would be just fine in the end because they were both in this together.

And for the first time Harry found himself starting to think that this was actually going to work out. Holly—his nerdy, practical, quiet archaeologist—made his world feel a better place simply because she was in it. She made him feel grounded.

This was crazy. They barely knew each other. She didn't even remember the night they'd spent together in Bath, thanks to her accident the day after. They'd been dating officially for all of three days. He couldn't possibly feel this way about her.

But just as she'd drawn his attention while he'd been playing the set at Bath, she drew him now. She made him feel centred.

'Sorry.' He kissed her back.

'First-time dad?' the woman next to them asked, an indulgent smile on her fact.

No. Not that he wanted to discuss that now. 'Yes,' he said. It wasn't a complete untruth. He and Rochelle hadn't made it as far as this stage.

'Don't worry. The scan won't hurt the baby, love, and it won't hurt your wife.' She patted her own bump. 'This one's our third. But my partner is still going to be here any minute now because nothing beats seeing your baby for the first time. It's magical.'

As if on cue, her partner arrived, but before she could introduce Harry and Holly to him, they were called into the ultrasound scan room.

'This is it.' Harry forced himself to hold Holly's hand in a supportive way rather than clutching it for dear life, and walked with her into the dimly lit ultrasound suite.

The sonographer talked them through the test; then Holly lay on the couch, lowered the waistband of her skirt and pulled up her top to expose the bump. The sonographer spread gel over Holly's stomach, and pressed the head of the probe against her abdomen.

And there, on the screen, was their baby.

'Say hello to your baby, Mr and Mrs Weston,' the sonographer said with a smile.

Harry didn't correct her that Holly was actually Dr Weston and he was Mr Moran. All he could see was a black and white screen, the baby's head and the curved spine.

'That's just one baby,' the sonographer said, then she took some measurements. 'When was your last menstrual period, Mrs Weston?'

Holly told her.

The sonographer smiled. 'Wonderful. It all ties up nicely with the measurements. You're fifteen weeks, so the baby is due at the end of February.'

Harry still couldn't speak. He just stared in wonder at the image on the screen.

'There are ten fingers and ten toes,' the sonographer continued. 'The heart is beating nice and strongly. I can't see anything that worries me at this stage, but I'll measure the fluid at the back of the baby's neck as part of the screening test.'

'Thank you,' Holly said.

She squeezed Harry's hand, and he realised he was meant to speak. 'Sorry. Thank you,' he mumbled. 'Sorry. I'm just…'

'The first time they see the baby blows most dads away,' the sonographer said kindly. 'Would you both like a photograph?'

'Yes, please,' he said. 'Our baby. I just…' He shook his head, as if barely able to believe what he was seeing. *Our baby.*

Harry actually had tears in his eyes, Holly realised, and her heart melted. She smiled at him. 'It's pretty amazing.'

'Fifteen weeks. So the baby is about the size of an apple, lanugo is covering the baby's skin, and they can hear your voice.'

The sonographer grinned. 'It sounds as if someone's been doing some bedtime reading, then.'

'A little bit,' Harry admitted.

When Holly had found out that she was pregnant, she'd been so sure that the baby's father wouldn't be in the slightest bit interested. From Harry's reaction just now, she knew that he was very much going to be a hands-on parent. They were in this together. She squeezed his hand again. 'That's good.'

The sonographer finished doing the measurements, printed out two photographs, and then Holly wiped off the gel and restored order to her clothes.

Harry couldn't stop looking at the photograph. 'Our baby,' he said again, his gorgeous blue eyes wide with wonder. Would their baby have his eyes? she wondered. What would their baby inherit from each of them? And she loved the idea that maybe they'd grow together as a family, see bits of themselves reflected in their child.

They headed for Trafalgar Square and through the National Gallery, discovering that their tastes in art were similar. After a quick lunch, they took their seats in St Martin's Church, and Holly thoroughly enjoyed the Mozart piano trios. Afterwards, Harry introduced her to his friends the performers, calling her his partner; it sent a weird little thrill through her veins.

'Are you going back to Beauchamp this afternoon?' he asked.

'This evening. I want to see my mum first,

and show her the picture of the baby,' Holly said. She looked at him. Was this rushing things too much? Then again, she and Simon had taken things really slowly and that hadn't worked out. Maybe she needed to be less cautious and do the opposite. 'If you don't have to rush off anywhere, then you're welcome to come with me.'

'I'd like that. And maybe I can drive you back to Beauchamp.'

'Thanks, but I'd rather have my car handy.'

'Then, if you don't mind giving me a lift, I'll get the train back from Cambridge tomorrow.' He paused. 'Right now, I want to tell the world about you and our baby, but I'll be guided by you on this.'

'We've been dating officially for all of three days,' she pointed out.

'We would've been dating for three months by now,' he countered, 'if things had gone according to our original plan.'

She looked at him. 'So you intend to be in this for the long haul?'

'We're still getting to know each other, and I made a mess of my marriage, so I don't want to make a promise and let you down,' he said, 'but whatever happens between you and me I intend to support you through pregnancy. And I'll be a hands-on dad.'

'You work away a lot,' she said. 'You can't be hands on from a distance.'

'As hands on as I can,' he amended. 'But, yes. If your parents want to know, my intentions towards you are entirely honourable. We're both capable of sorting out the complicated stuff between us, even if it takes a little time.' He kissed her lightly. 'I don't think either of us expected this. But we'll make it work.'

'It scares the hell out of me,' she admitted. 'I knew Simon for years. I thought we were fine. And it all went wrong.'

'Whereas we've done everything the wrong way round,' he said. 'So maybe this time it'll go right.'

How could she explain that she was punching so far above her weight, being with him? She hadn't been enough for Simon, and he was a dull accountant. How could she possibly be enough for an award-winning musician who led an incredibly glamorous life crisis-crossing the globe?

To her horror, she realised she'd spoken some of it aloud, because Harry raised an eyebrow.

'Let me unpick this for you. Firstly, your ex doesn't sound like a very nice guy, so don't look at yourself through his eyes. Secondly, my life isn't that glamorous. Although

I dress up for a performance, there's a lot of time spent travelling, checking lighting and seating, waiting around, and practising scales. Thirdly, I never get distracted when I'm working, with the exception of Bath—so there's something about you that's special. The more time I spend with you, the more I like you. So stop worrying about whether you're enough, because you *are*.'

It brought a lump in her throat, to the point where she couldn't answer.

He kissed her again. 'If it makes you feel any better, I'm pretty nervous about meeting your mum. In her shoes, I'd want to know exactly why this gadabout, flaky guy made my daughter pregnant and deserted her.'

'I didn't remember anything about you and you didn't have enough information to get in touch with me,' she reminded him. 'So it's not quite desertion.'

'It is, if you think about it. I could've tried to search for you on social media.'

'I would've *hated* that,' she said. 'So I'm glad you didn't.'

'Even so. I'm meeting your mum for the first time, and I can't possibly go without flowers—seriously nice flowers,' he said, and insisted on stopping at a florist's on the way back to Camden.

* * *

Ginny Weston was delighted by the flowers, but even more so by the way Harry behaved towards her younger daughter. 'The way he looks at you—Simon never looked at you like that,' she said quietly to Holly in the kitchen.

Holly flushed. 'Mum!'

'I know, I know. It's early days, and you've both got the baby to think about—and he must still be coming to terms with the fact that he's going to be a dad. But the way he looks at you... That's exactly how I want your partner to look at you,' she said. 'If he hadn't taken your number down wrong, he would've been there at your bedside the whole time while you were in hospital.'

'No, he wouldn't. He was working the next day.'

'I have a feeling he would've made some alternative arrangements to make sure he was there by your side,' Ginny said. 'I like him.'

They stopped long enough that Harry ended up meeting Holly's father and sister, too. And Natalie, who had texted to ask about the scan and dropped in on her way home from work. So it was much, much later than Holly had intended by the time they got to Beauchamp.

'You've been a hit with my family and my

best friend,' she said. She swallowed hard. 'But although yours seem to like me in my professional capacity—'

'—they'll love you as my partner and the mother of my child,' Harry finished. 'Ellen and Dominic are lovely. My parents are difficult, yes, but you might already have worked out for yourself that the trick to dealing with them is to ignore whatever they say.' He paused. 'Granny Beckett would've asked you a lot of questions. And then she would've smiled and given you the biggest hug.' He smiled. 'So don't worry. My family and closest friends will approve of you.'

Just for a second, there was something in his expression that she couldn't read. What wasn't he telling her?

'It's your choice,' he said, squeezing her hand. 'You can drop me here outside Nell's and we'll tell her tomorrow if you want to get some rest. Or we can tell her now, if you're going to lie awake worrying about it all night.'

'I wasn't a worrier until the hormones started,' she said.

'Are they going to keep you awake tonight?'

She nodded ruefully.

'Then let's face the music tonight,' he said, 'because you need to rest properly.'

He held her hand all the way down the garden path, and he was still holding her hand when his sister answered the door.

'Harry! We weren't expecting you tonight.' Then Ellen noticed him holding hands with Holly. 'Oh. Nice to see you, too, Holly.'

'Can we come in?' Harry asked.

'Of course. I'll put the kettle on.' She smiled at them. 'I wish I'd known you were going to call in tonight. George and Alice are asleep and they'll be so upset to have missed you.'

'They'll see me tomorrow, if you don't mind me scrounging a bed,' Harry said.

'Of course not.' She rolled her eyes at him. 'You know we always have room for you.'

'I have news,' Harry said, and proceeded to tell Ellen everything.

Holly's breathing grew more and more shallow, and adrenaline rather than blood seem to be flowing through her veins.

But when Harry had finished, Ellen just grinned and hugged her. 'Well, obviously it's all a big surprise and it's a bit complicated—but I'm so pleased for you both and I really hope you've got a scan picture of my niece-or-nephew-to-be, because I'm dying to see it!'

And from that moment on it was all easy. Ellen persuaded Harry to video-call Dominic and Sally and explain it to them, and they seemed just as pleased as Ellen and Tristan were.

'One thing, though,' Sally said. 'If you two decide to get married, you really need to have "Don't You Forget About Me" as your first dance.'

'Or anything from Radiohead's *Amnesiac*,' Dominic chipped in.

Harry groaned. 'This one is going to run and run, isn't it?'

'Absolutely. Oh, and you need forget-me-nots in your bouquet. Welcome to the family, Holly,' Dominic said. 'So when are you telling the parents, Harry?'

'Tomorrow,' Harry said.

'If they say anything vile, Holly, just ignore them,' Dominic said. 'And be assured that we'll all have your back when Harry's not here.'

'So you don't all think I'm…' Holly's voice faded.

'We think,' Ellen said, 'you're sensible, you're lovely, the kids adore you, and you're perfect for our baby brother.'

The Viscount and Viscountess were too taken aback to say anything rude when Harry told them the news the next morning. And Harry forwarded a slew of texts from the rest of the quartet to Holly, saying they were looking forward to meeting Harry's mysterious Lady in Red at last. The fact that he'd clearly talked about her to his closes friends, even when he hadn't known who she was, reassured her.

Although Harry had to head off on Thursday, he called Holly every single day, texted her snippets about what new developments their baby would have that week, sent her a photograph of the gorgeous hotel where the quartet we are playing on the Saturday, and picked her up on Sunday to take her to lunch at Lucy and Carina's so she could meet his closest friends and colleagues.

'This is just brilliant,' Lucy said, hugging her warmly. 'I'm so glad he's met someone like you.'

'The woman who forgot him the very next day?' Holly asked wryly.

'That wasn't your fault. What were you supposed to do, let that idiot drive straight into a little boy? Actually, I think you were really brave, scooping him up like that.'

'Instinct,' Holly said. 'Anyone would've done the same.'

'Actually, a lot of people wouldn't have had the nerve.' Lucy tucked her arm through Holly's. 'Right. Let's get you a drink, a decent seat, and something to eat. Do you play an instrument at all?'

'I'm sorry, no. I just listen to music.'

'Don't apologise.' Lucy smiled brightly.

Was it her imagination, Holly wondered, or did Lucy look relieved?

'Though Harry taught me to do a round of "Frère Jacques" at the piano with his niece and nephew. And he got me to sing—you know, the bit in *Truly Madly Deeply*.'

'I love that film. It makes me cry buckets,' Lucy said. 'But if you're encouraging him to play the cello like a guitar...'

Holly bit her lip, remembering what Harry had said about how his colleagues viewed that style of playing. 'Sorry.'

Lucy chuckled. 'I'm teasing. Our Harry doesn't need encouragement. Actually, I've seen a huge difference him over the last week—a difference that makes us all very happy—and it's all thanks to you.'

The next couple of weeks were more of the same: seeing Harry in London on Sundays and on the occasional evening if he could get down to Beauchamp.

'You're my Sunday girl,' he teased, the evening when they were curled up together on his sofa, and hummed the middle section of Blondie's 'Sunday Girl'.

'If you start playing that on the cello, the quartet will have my guts for garters,' she said with a grin.

'Are you kidding? They adore you.' He paused.

Her heart skipped a beat. Was he going to say he adored her, too?

'Holly, I...' Then he stopped.

What was holding him back? Worry that she didn't feel the same?

'I don't want to rush you,' he said, 'but I can't help myself. I apologise in advance. But I...' He rolled his eyes. 'Sorry. I'm usually good with words.'

But not when it came to emotional stuff? Maybe it would help if she said it first. 'You're adorable,' she said. Though she wasn't going to say the L word. It was too soon. Though she knew she was falling harder for Harry with every day that passed.

'That's how I feel about you, too,' he said, as if she'd spoken her thoughts aloud. 'Do you have to go home tonight?'

Her pulse leapt. 'You're asking me to stay?'

'Yes. And I'll drive you home tomorrow. Whatever time you like,' he said. 'Though if I'm rushing you, I'll wait.' He stroked her hair. 'I just don't want to say goodnight.'

She didn't either. She missed him hugely when they weren't together, and it was good to know that he felt the same.

Yes, this was rushing it. Then again, she was carrying his baby. So maybe none of the conventions mattered any more. 'I'll stay,' she said.

He kissed her lingeringly. 'Good. Because I want to wake up with you in my arms.'

Just as she presumed they'd done in Bath.

'I really hate the fact,' she said, 'that I don't remember Bath. That I don't remember making our baby.'

Colour slashed through his face. 'Obviously I didn't know we were making a baby at the time, but I definitely remember making love with you.' His eyes held a bright, almost febrile glitter. 'Maybe if we repeat it, your memory will come back.'

She didn't think it would. Not now.

Clearly it showed in her expression, because he said, 'Even if it doesn't, I'll do my best to make it the same.'

It didn't bring her memory back, but Holly loved the way that Harry let her undress him, clearly keeping himself in check. Even in jeans, he was gorgeous; out of them, he was even more so, his musculature sculpted and his abdomen flat.

'You're so beautiful,' she whispered.

'Thank you. But I'm feeling a bit under-dressed now. My turn?' Harry asked.

Feeling ridiculously shy, she nodded and let him undress her. He took it slowly, ca-ressing every centimetre of skin he uncov-ered, until her whole body felt heated. He lingered particularly over her abdomen. 'I can see the changes in you,' he said, 'and you're gorgeous.'

'I'm very ordinary,' she corrected.

'Are you, hell,' he said. He scooped her up and carried her to his bed. 'Simon might have had blinkers, but I don't. You once told me you were beige. Well, you're not. You're gold and honey—the colour of your hair, the colour of your eyes, the way the sun kisses your skin.'

And then he proceeded to show her just how gorgeous he thought she was.

Afterwards, she lay curled in his arms, sated. 'I still don't see how a bang on the head could make me forget something as amazing as that. Someone as amazing as you.'

'Memory is a funny thing. And it's bound up in all the senses. Like Proust and his madeleines,' he said thoughtfully, 'the scent and taste bringing the memory back.'

'I guess.' She kissed him. 'I'm just sorry I forgot you. Because you're not at all forgettable.'

'And I'm sorry I didn't just suck it up and do the whole "Help me find my Lady in Red" thing on social media,' he said. 'Because I hate to think you believed I would ever desert you.'

'That isn't who you are,' she said. 'You know I'm glad you didn't do the social media stuff! I'd hate to have people gawping over my private life.'

'Then it's just as well I work in the area I do, rather than rock or pop,' Harry said. 'We get a lot less press intrusion.' He curled his hand round her abdomen. 'Right now, all I can think of is you, me and our baby.'

She stilled.

'What's wrong?' Harry asked.

'I think,' she said, 'I just felt the baby move. Like bubbles inside me.'

'I read that it could happen around this time,' he said thoughtfully. 'But it will be a while before I can feel the baby move.'

'You really have been reading up,' she said, smiling.

'I have. And I'm hoping you'll let me come

to your antenatal classes. I mean it about supporting you.' He kissed her again. 'And I'd
like to start playing music to our baby. Music
is meant to be good for helping you relax and
bond with the baby, and for the structure of
the baby's brain. Plus studies show the the that
babies actually remember the music they hear
in the womb.'

'Sounds good to me. And I'd like to read
those studies, too,' she said. 'Let me have
the link.'

'I will.' He smiled. 'Thank you for indulg-
ing me in the nerdy stuff.'

'No problem. I'm sure Amenhotep or
Nefertiti will enjoy you playing to them.'

He stared at her. 'Amenhotep and Nefertiti? They're the names you've picked out?'

'But of course. My favourite pharaoh and
the most beautiful woman in the world,' she
said, enjoying the expression on his face—
a mingled look of horror and a desperate at-
tempt to be supportive.

'Amen...' He blew out a breath. Then the
penny clearly dropped. 'All right. Ammy or
Nef it is.'

He'd even worked out the diminutives?

'As long as we have a middle name of
Camille for a boy and Hildegard for a girl,'
he added.

He'd lost her as much as she'd lost him. 'Camille?' she asked.

'Saint-Saëns,' he explained.

The composer of one of the most famous cello pieces, she remembered. 'And Hildegard?'

'Of Bingen. She was a twelfth-century Benedictine abbess, composer, writer and philosopher,' he explained.

Holly laughed. 'I've already horrified my best friend. I'm so looking forward to seeing her face when she hears *your* suggestions.'

He laughed and kissed her. 'I guess we have some more serious decisions to make, but we have plenty of time. For now, I want to enjoy just being with you.'

CHAPTER NINE

BY THE MIDDLE of October, Holly began to believe that this was going to work out. Although Harry's schedule was hectic, he was scrupulous about coming to antenatal classes and appointments with her. He saw her every Sunday and as many other days in the week as he could, and on the days when he was away working he video-called her and played a lullaby to the baby.

The day he felt the baby kick for the first time, Harry went uncharacteristically quiet. Holly reminded herself that they were still getting to know each other, still getting used to their back-to-front situation. Just because she was starting to fall in love with him, it didn't mean that he was falling in love with her. And, although Harry had been vocal on the subject of Simon's behaviour towards her, deep inside Holly still worried that she wasn't going to be enough for him. Would he grow bored? Would he feel that she was holding him back? Would he expect her to put her career second to his—especially as he'd already warned her that he'd put his career before his marriage?

Once she'd let herself think, the worries multiplied. She didn't know where to start unpicking them and discussing them with Harry so, not wanting to rock the boat, she said nothing.

But if there was a time to say those three little words, when emotion was bubbling high, she thought it would be the moment after he felt the baby kick. The fact that he hadn't said it... Was he with her because he felt obliged to be there, rather than wanting to be with her?

The thought wouldn't go away. She needed to be careful. Last time round, she'd loved Simon more than he'd loved her and she'd ended up hurt. She couldn't let herself love Harry until he was sure how she felt he felt about her. And she certainly wasn't going to be the one to say it first. She had her pride.

This was a tightrope, Harry thought. One he'd negotiated before and he'd fallen off. Been badly hurt.

Could he take the risk that this time he would stay sure-footed?

But the parallels between the past and the present worried him. He'd married Rochelle because she'd been pregnant. It had been a knee-jerk reaction because he'd loved her and had wanted to support her. He and Rochelle had had a lot in common, similar careers, had known each other for years and had always got on well, and the sex had been good. So on paper their marriage should've worked out. They should've been strong enough to cope with the miscarriage, help each other through it.

Instead, everything had collapsed. He'd discovered that she hadn't really loved him—she'd loved the idea of being part of an aristocratic family, but she hadn't loved him for himself.

This time round, the way he felt about Holly was nothing like he'd ever felt for anyone before. OK, so they hadn't known each other long, and for a lot of that time she'd forgotten he even existed, thanks to her amnesia, but they were working on it. It wasn't just sexual attraction: he really liked the woman he was getting to know. He was pretty sure he was in love with her. And he'd almost told her that when he'd felt the baby kick.

But how could he be sure that it would work this time?

He didn't want to upset Holly with his doubts, so he said nothing. Maybe his doubts would go. Maybe he just needed a little more time.

On Sunday, the quartet was due to fly to Berlin to play three nights of Mozart. They had arranged to have a late lunch at Lucy's house before the flight, and both Carina and Holly planned to wave the quartet off at the airport.

'You're really blooming, Holly,' Lucy said, 'and Harry looks so happy. It's lovely to see that. Especially after Roch—' She stopped abruptly, her eyes widening with obvious horror. 'I'm so sorry. I didn't mean to put my foot in it.'

'It's OK. I know about Rochelle,' Holly reassured her. She was beginning to think that the divorce was one of the reasons why Harry might be holding back, scared of repeating a mistake.

'I'm glad he told you. Though I did worry a bit when he first told us about you.' Lucy bit her lip. 'Especially because of the baby. It was so sad.'

Sad? What was sad? What baby? Was Lucy telling her that Harry had a child he didn't see? Holly stared at her, shocked. 'Baby?' she asked finally.

Lucy winced. 'Just ignore me. I'm talking rubbish.'

'I don't think you are. And I'd rather know the truth,' Holly said. 'Otherwise my imagination will blow it up into something far worse.'

'Sorry.' Lucy squeezed her hand. 'I don't know how to say this without upsetting you. It's just about the worst thing you can possibly say to a pregnant woman. Rochelle, um, had a miscarriage, just before the dating scan.'

Holly went cold. A miscarriage. OK, so she was beyond the twelve-week mark now, so the risk was an awful lot lower; but was this why Harry was holding back, because he was scared that history might repeat itself?

And why hadn't he told her? It was another lie of omission, and it made her wonder what else he was keeping from her. When she thought about it, it hadn't been just an omission; he'd out-and-out lied about it, telling the woman in the waiting room at the scan that he was a first-time father.

Clearly he that wasn't true.

Now she was going to question everything he said to her, and that wasn't good.

'Holly? Are you all right?' Lucy asked, looking concerned.

'I'm fine,' Holly fibbed. 'Just a bit tired.'

'If you want to go and have a lie down, you're welcome to have a nap in our spare bedroom,' Lucy said.

What Holly really wanted was her own space. Time to think about what she'd just learned and what it meant for her future. If Harry wasn't going to trust her with the whole truth of his past, it wasn't going to work between them. Was he really over his ex and the loss of their child? Was he only with *her* because she was expecting his baby and he felt obliged to stay with her?

'That's really kind of you,' she said, 'but I'll be fine.'

Somehow she managed to make small talk with Harry's friends during the rest of lunch, and then she insisted that she and Harry would do the washing up together.

'Can we have a quiet word?' she asked when they were halfway through.

He frowned. 'Sure. What's wrong?'

There was no point in pussyfooting about. She needed to know the truth. 'When were you going to tell me about Rochelle's baby?'

He blanched. 'Oh, Christ. Who told you?'

'It doesn't matter—the person concerned

thought I already knew. And you should've told me a long time ago.' She scrubbed the last few plates a bit too hard. 'Harry, you're clearly with me just because you feel obliged to be with me.'

He looked aghast. 'That's not true.'

But she didn't believe him. And she didn't want to be with someone who was selective with the truth. Been there, done that, and worn the T-shirt. 'I'm going home to my flat when I've done the washing up,' she said. 'On my own. Maybe we'll talk when you get back from Berlin and you've had time to think about what you really want.'

'But—'

'No buts,' she cut in, as gently as she could. 'I don't know what else you've been keeping from me.'

'I haven't kept anything from you.'

'Lies of omission are still lies, Harry. I had enough lies from Simon to last me a lifetime, and I can't spend the rest of my days wondering if you're keeping me in the dark about something.'

'Holly, I'm—'

'When you're back from Berlin,' she cut in. 'We'll talk then. But right now I don't want to see you. I need some space. Please thank Lucy and Carina for their hospitality. I'm going now, without any fuss.' Even though it was ripping her apart. Even though she'd planned to go to the airport with Harry and wave him off, she couldn't bear to do that now.

And just like that Harry's world switched into monochrome. Even though it was an unseasonably warm autumn afternoon, it felt like a dull winter's evening.

How could this all have gone so wrong?'

One thing he did know: there was no way he was letting Holly go.

He went to find Lucy. 'Holly's a bit tired,' he said, 'so she's slipped off home, but she wanted me to say thank you for her.'

'I'm really sorry that I dropped you in it,' Lucy said, biting her lip. 'I thought you'd told her about Rochelle.'

'Not about the miscarriage,' Harry said. 'Given that Holly's pregnant, it's not exactly a good subject.'

'I'm sorry if I caused a row between you.

'You didn't do it on purpose,' Harry said.

'But?' she asked.

He sighed. 'But she said she doesn't want to talk to me until we get back from Berlin. Lucy, I know this is all last minute, but—'

'You don't want to go to Berlin with us,' she finished.

'Holly's not like Rochelle. She didn't give me any ultimatums,' he said. 'But I really can't go until I've fixed this.'

'Our flight's this evening,' Lucy reminded him.

'But we're not actually playing until tomorrow evening. I can book another flight for me for tomorrow morning,' Harry said. 'I know it's going to mess up rehearsals, and I'm sorry.'

'I guess it'll mess things up more if your head's all over the place. We'll manage. Go after her,' Lucy advised. 'But just keep us posted about what's happening tomorrow.'

'I will.' He hugged her. 'Thanks.'

Except, when Harry turned up at Holly's flat, she wasn't there. And her phone went straight through to voicemail.

He sat on her doorstep. She'd told him that she was going back to her flat. Where else would she have gone? The most likely places were to her parents or to Natalie, but he didn't want to risk going to the wrong place and missing her.

He pulled out his phone and called Natalie. As he'd half expected, she didn't pick up.

She might be able to ignore a call, but she'd see a message. And hopefully she'd pass it on.

Please tell Holly I'm sitting on her doorstep and I've cancelled my flight.

He waited.
No response.
He gave it another ten minutes before he sent a second text.

And I'm not moving until she talks to me, even if I have to sit here for the entire night.

That did the trick, because his phone shrilled and Holly's name came up on the screen. 'You're being melodramatic and ridiculous,' she said crossly.

'No,' he said quietly. 'Actually, I'm just desperate. And I'll do whatever it takes so you'll talk to me about this. Preferably face to face.'

'Go home, Harry.'

'I don't want to go to Berlin and leave things like this between us. Please. Come and talk to me, Holly.'

'Is there any point?'

'I think so. But how will you know unless you hear what I have to say?'

There was a long, long pause, and for a

nasty moment Harry thought he'd pushed her too far and she'd call the whole thing off. But finally she said, 'I'll give you twenty minutes.'

'Thank you.'

It was forty minutes until the black cab dropped her outside.

'Why are you doing this?' she asked.

'I can't go to Berlin and leave things like this between us,' he said.

'It's your *job*,' she pointed out. 'You're supposed to play for three nights. You can't just not turn up.'

'I'll get the redeye flight tomorrow—*if* we've sorted this out.'

'Then I suppose you'd better come in.' She unlocked the door and ushered him inside.

'I'm sorry,' he said. 'I know how you feel about lying. I honestly didn't intend to hide anything from you.' He grimaced. 'I didn't tell you about the miscarriage because you're pregnant and I didn't want to worry you. I did intend to tell you about it—but there never seemed to be a good time.'

Holly folded her arms. 'Try now. I'm listening.'

'I'll tell you the truth. All of it. But this isn't very nice,' he warned. 'I told you I was married. What I didn't tell you was that although I thought I loved Rochelle at the time, the main reason I married her was because she told me she was pregnant. The baby wasn't planned.'

Just like *their* baby. No wonder Harry hadn't let her close. He'd obviously thought he was making the same mistake all over again.

She swallowed hard and kept listening.

'Rochelle was having trouble finding work, and I knew she wanted security for the baby, so we got a licence and married as soon as possible in the registry office. It wasn't a big do: just the two of us and a couple of strangers who agreed to be our witnesses. I went on tour, promising to do the honeymoon bit and whisk her away when I got back. Except I didn't because, two days before the dating scan—while I was still away—she lost the baby.'

'I'm sorry,' Holly said. 'That must've been horrible for both of you.'

'It was.' He dragged in a breath. 'I wasn't there for her. The quartet was only just taking off so I couldn't just ask someone else to play in my stead. I didn't want to let the others down, and I knew her mum was there with her so I thought it would be OK to carry on with the tour.' He raked a hand through his hair. 'It seems absolutely insane to me now.

Why on earth didn't I catch the first flight home? It was terrible of me. To be honest, I don't think I knew how to confront my own grief about it all. But that marked the beginning of the end for us.'

Holly's heart bled for him and for his ex. It sounded as if they'd married in haste and really repented at leisure—and they'd both had to deal with losing a baby, too. Without realising what she was doing, she splayed her fingers protectively against her abdomen.

'Exactly,' Harry said wryly, clearly noticing what she'd done. 'That's why I didn't tell you. I knew it would upset you.'

It wasn't just that. He hadn't been honest about the end of his marriage either. 'You led to me to believe it was the pressure of your careers that drove you apart,' she said.

'It was, in part.' Harry looked at her. 'Losing the baby just made the cracks wider. She wanted me to give up my music and go to work in the family business.'

'But you would've *hated* that.'

He nodded. 'It just got worse and worse. We had a massive fight and she told me to choose between her and the quartet. I couldn't believe she was actually asking me to give up who I am.' He swallowed hard. 'I've never told anyone this bit before, but that was when she told me the truth. Something that hurt like hell, but ironically made it easy for me to make the decision. She told me that she'd deliberately got pregnant because she knew it'd make me marry her. She thought it would give her financial security and make her part of an aristocratic family.' He closed his eyes briefly. 'She didn't love me for *me*. She loved the youngest son of Viscount Moran. My career wasn't enough for her; she wanted all the glitz and glamour that went with my family, or so she thought. So that made the decision easy. I said I was a musician first. And she said she wanted a divorce.'

Holly absorbed the news. Rochelle had deliberately got pregnant? She'd seen Harry as a means of security, rather than him being the love of her life? That put a whole new spin on things. No wonder Harry was shy of relationships. Maybe, just like her, he thought he wasn't enough for anyone.

But she also knew the last thing he wanted was pity. She'd hated all the pity, too. 'That's rough,' she said. 'And I'm sorry she saw you like that. You're worth a lot more. And that's not pity talking, by the way.'

'I know. You've been there yourself.' He looked away for a moment. 'You can't get divorced in England on the grounds of irreconcilable differences. We went to a solicitor. Neither of us had committed adultery, so that left us with the option of citing unreasonable behaviour.' He grimaced. 'Mine.'

'That's not fair,' she said.

He shrugged. 'It was that, or agreeing to separate and then waiting for two years. Besides, she had a point. I hadn't behaved well. I should've been there for her when she lost the baby instead of wrapping myself in the security of my music.'

'She didn't exactly behave well, either,' Holly pointed out.

He shook his head. 'I'm not playing the blame game. I've seen my parents do that too many times and it doesn't end well for anyone. Maybe she feels guilty now about the way she treated me—I don't know. But we were both to blame. And we both wanted out of the marriage. But after that I swore I'd never get involved with anyone again.' He looked at her. 'What I didn't expect was to meet you. To fall in love with you.'

She felt her eyes widen. '*Do* you love me?'

'I love you,' he confirmed.

He'd said it first. But he didn't look happy about it.

'And it scares the hell out of me,' he added. 'Because you're in almost the same situation again—an unplanned baby, but this time with someone you haven't known for years?'

'No,' he said. 'It doesn't matter about not knowing you for very long and it doesn't matter that we didn't plan the baby. What scares me is that something might go wrong with our baby like it did with mine and Rochelle's baby. With music, I know what I'm doing and how to fix problems, but with a baby… I have no control over what happens.'

'I'm past the most dangerous trimester,' she said gently. 'And, despite the horror stories you see in the news, most pregnancies and births are straightforward.' She looked at him. She knew she was going to have to ask the hardest question, for her own peace of mind. 'Do you still love Rochelle?'

'No. I did, back then. At least, I thought I did at the time. But now I'm not sure I did, because the way I feel about you isn't the same as I felt about her. I love you. I know I do. You make the world feel grounded. But I'm still scared.' He looked anguished. 'What if I'm a terrible father?'

'Because your own parents weren't great with you, you mean?'

'Yes.'

'You're not them, Harry. You'll do things differently.'

'How can you know?'

'Because of your grandmother,' she said. 'I think that's the sort of parenting that will stick with you. Someone who notices, someone who makes a difference. Someone who gives, someone who guides without being pushy. And from what I've seen, you're an excellent uncle.'

He inclined his head in acknowledgement. 'Thank you, but there's a huge difference between looking after my nieces and nephews for a little while and being responsible for a baby full time. What if I get things wrong?'

'You muddle through and you work it out.' She looked at him. 'Just like you said to Henry and Celia when they were playing for you—if you make a mistake, you smile and keep going. You learn not to make the same mistake next time.'

'I know I'm not making the same mistake I made with Rochelle. I love you, Holly. I want to be with you. I want to live with you and make a family with you. But I'm scared you'll think I'm only saying that because of the baby.'

She knew they needed to face that one head on. 'Are you?'

He shook his head. 'We didn't plan our baby, but he or she definitely isn't unwanted.

I want to be a good dad and I want to be there for our baby—but I'm asking you to marry me for *my* sake. I want to be with you, Holly, but I'm trying not to pressure you.' He paused. 'So I'll ask you: what do you want?'

'I still don't remember meeting you for the first time, and maybe I never will,' she said. 'And when I met you at Beauchamp I thought you were a spoiled poor little rich boy.'

'And then?'

'Then I started getting to know you. And I liked the man I was spending time with. You're good with children, you're fun to be around, and you play the cello so beautifully that you make me cry.' She took a deep breath. 'I'm scared that you only want to marry me because you feel you ought to. I'm ordinary. If I wasn't enough for Simon, how can I possibly be enough for you?'

He walked over to her and wrapped his arms round her. 'Because you're everything I want. You make me feel as if the world's a good place. You're the only woman I've ever noticed while I'm playing—and until now music has been my main focus in life.' He stole a kiss.

'But now I want more. I want you, and I want to be a family with you. And I know I've messed up twice now by not telling you something because I was trying to protect you, but I've learnt from my mistakes. You don't need me to be your knight in shining armour. You're perfectly capable of sorting everything out yourself—except you don't have to. I'll be there with you. All the way. I'll tell you everything, even if I have to warn you first that it's the wrong time or the wrong place or I'm concerned that it might hurt you. Because I know how much you value honesty—and I honestly, honestly love you, Holly.'

'I love you, too,' she said. 'And I'm never going to make you choose between me and your music.'

'So what do you want?' he asked.

'Love. Honesty. Fairness,' she said. 'I'm not expecting the future to be easy. You're away a lot, and my job's going to take me away from London from time to time. I want the baby and my career.'

'That's what I want, too. So we'll compromise,' he said. 'I'll tour less. I could teach.'

'Would you be happy teaching?' she asked. 'Because there's a big difference between finding a workable compromise and making yourself unhappy. And I can definitely assure you that I don't want you to give things up and work at Beauchamp. I like your family—even your parents, actually, because they're all right with me—but it's not the right place for you. You're a musician.'

'Thank you,' he said, 'for understanding. I don't know if teaching's for me, but this is a good point to rethink the direction of my career.' He looked thoughtful. 'I'd like to try composing. Writing music for films. I could do that from home and we can share the baby's care between us—and make time for us, too.'

'We could schedule it,' she said. 'The baby. Work. Date night.'

There was a distinct twinkle in his eyes. 'Says my gorgeously nerdy academic. I like that idea.'

'So we're going to live together, as a family?'

'Yes. Though we need to find a house. My flat's too small for the three of us.'

'So's mine,' she said.

'So we'll go house-hunting tomorrow.'

'We'll go house-hunting,' she said, 'when you're back from Berlin. Speaking of which, you really do need to go. You'll miss your flight.'

'I already cancelled it. I can book the first flight out tomorrow morning,' he said, 'or I could try to find someone else to take my place in Berlin.'

'That isn't fair on Lucy, Stella or Drew,' she pointed out. 'Go to Berlin.'

'Provided you forgive me for not telling you about the baby earlier?'

'Only because I hope you've learnt not to lie by omission.'

'I have,' he said. 'So now that's cleared up, can we go for a walk?'

She folded her arms. '*After* you've booked your flight.'

'Give me ten minutes,' he said, and grabbed his phone from his pocket. He booked the flight and tapped in his credit card details. 'All organised. It's the first flight tomorrow. If I check in an hour before the flight, I need to leave here by about half-past four in the morning.'

'I'll drive you to the airport,' she said.

'You need your sleep.'

She shook her head. 'I'll be awake anyway. Amenhotep seems to wake up at half-past three to do a bit of baby gymnastics.'

'Noted,' he said. 'And I'll do my share of night feeds for Amenhotep Camille.'

'I'll hold you to that,' she said with a grin.

'Now can we go for that walk?'

'What's so special about a walk?'

'Humour me?' he asked softly.

She rolled her eyes, but let him lead her out

of the house and out to Primrose Hill. At the top, they paused to look at the view.

'The whole of London before us,' he said softly.

And then he dropped to one knee.

'Holly Weston, I love you. I think I might even have fallen in love with you before you remembered knowing me. It scares the hell out of me because I've never felt this way about anyone before, but not having you in my life is an even more scary prospect. I'm not promising that it's going to be easy, but I'll be honest with you and I'll love you for the rest of my days, and I'll try to be the best husband and father I can possibly be. Will you marry me?'

'I love you, too,' she said. 'Even if I did forget you the day after I met you. Yes, I'll marry you.'

EPILOGUE

April

'YOU'RE READY FOR THIS?' Holly's father checked.

'I'm ready,' she said with a smile. 'Mum's got Eliot?'

'And he's sound asleep,' her father said, smiling back.

'I still can't believe you're making everyone wear Regency dress. And that you're getting married in a red dress, too,' Natalie said, making a last-minute adjustment to Holly's bonnet and veil.

'It's where it all started,' Holly said. 'I don't remember wearing a dress like this—and, anyway, Harry looks amazing in full Regency garb. We kind of had to.' Just as she'd insisted on having forget-me-nots in her bouquet and woven into her hair.

Natalie grinned. 'I'm not complaining!

I love my dress. And the children all look so cute.'

Alice and Celia were flower girls, and Henry and George were ushers, all taking their duties incredibly seriously.

The wedding was in the family's private chapel at Beauchamp Abbey. As Holly's father opened the door and led her inside, Holly could see that Lucy, Drew and Stella were waiting to play her down the aisle. She suppressed a grin. Harry had thought she'd asked for Pachelbel's Canon; the rest of the quartet had had other ideas, aided and abetted by Harry's sister-in-law.

Celia and Alice walked down the aisle in front of the bride and her father, scattering rose petals, and at Holly's nod the trio switched from Pachelbel and started playing 'Don't You Forget About Me'.

Harry turned to watch her walk down the aisle to him, grinning broadly as he recognised the tune, and there was a ripple of amusement and love throughout the congregation, who all knew exactly why she was walking down the aisle to that particular tune.

In a red Regency dress, to a man wearing a tailcoat and pantaloons.

And then it hit her.

She remembered.

She remembered Harry wearing the Regency outfit and striding across the lawn to her. She remembered him putting his jacket round her shoulders. She remembered him walking her to the house and dancing with her, making her feel as if she were floating on air. She remembered him playing the cello to her, playing this exact tune, then dancing with her again. Asking her to stay with him. Carrying her across the threshold of his bedroom, making her feel precious and cherished and gorgeous.

Every step she took down the aisle towards him brought back another memory, another feeling, until her head was full of rainbows and she was close to tears of joy.

'Holly?' he asked, looking concerned when she joined him at the aisle.

'I remember,' she said. 'I remember the first time I met you, and you played me this exact song in Ferdy's wonderful Georgian flat. I was wearing a red dress, like this one, and you were wearing Regency clothes, just like you are now, and you made me feel amazing. I *remember*.' She blinked back the tears.

'I'm glad I made you feel amazing, because you *are* amazing.' He dipped his head and stole a kiss. 'And I'm glad you remember. Because right now my heart's beating as fast as it did the very first time I saw you, and I can't wait to marry you—because I really, really love you.'

'I really, really love you, too—and I won't forget you again,' she promised.

The vicar, who had baptised Harry as a baby—and who'd baptised Harry and Holly's baby the previous Sunday—smiled at them both. 'That's good to hear. Now, your guests are waiting.' He coughed, and raised his voice. 'Dearly beloved, we are gathered here…'

* * * * *

If you enjoyed this story,
check out these other great reads from
Kate Hardy

Soldier's Prince's Secret Baby Gift
Finding Mr. Right in Florence
A Diamond in the Snow
Reunited at the Altar

All available now!